Contents

I

A few miles south of Soledad[1], the Salinas River drops in[2] close to the hillside bank[3] and runs deep and green. The water is warm too, for it has slipped twinkling[4] over the yellow sands in the sunlight before reaching the narrow pool[5]. On one side of the river the golden foothill slopes[6] curve up to the strong and rocky Gabilan mountains, but on the valley side the water is lined with trees—willows[7] fresh and green with every spring, carrying in their lower leaf junctures the debris of the winter's flooding[8]; and sycamores with mottled[9], white, recumbent limbs[10] and branches that arch over the pool. On the sandy bank[11] under the trees the leaves lie deep and so crisp[12] that a lizard makes a great skittering[13] if he runs among them. Rabbits come out of the brush[14] to sit on the sand in the evening, and the damp flats[15] are covered with the night tracks of 'coons[16], and with the spread pads of dogs from the ranches, and with the split-wedge tracks of deer[17] that come to drink in the dark.

There is a path through the willows and among the sycamores, a path beaten hard[18] by boys coming down from the ranches to swim in the deep pool, and beaten hard by tramps[19] who come wearily[20] down from the highway in the evening to jungle-up[21] near water. In front of the low horizontal limb[22] of a giant sycamore there is an ash pile made by many fires; the limb is worn smooth[23] by men who have sat on it.

Evening of a hot day started the little wind to moving among the leaves. The shade climbed up[24] the

6

hills toward the top. On the sand banks the rabbits sat as quietly as little gray, sculptured stones. And then from the direction of the state highway came the sound of footsteps on crisp sycamore leaves. The rabbits hurried noiselessly for cover. A stilted[1] heron labored up into the air and pounded down river[2]. For a moment the place was lifeless, and then two men emerged from the path and came into the opening by the green pool.

They had walked in single file[3] down the path, and even in the open one stayed behind the other. Both were dressed in denim trousers and in denim coats with brass[4] buttons. Both wore black, shapeless[5] hats and both carried tight blanket rolls slung over[6] their shoulders. The first man was small and quick, dark of face, with restless eyes[7] and sharp, strong features[8]. Every part of him was defined: small, strong hands, slender arms[9], a thin and bony[10] nose. Behind him walked his opposite, a huge man, shapeless of face, with large, pale eyes, with wide, sloping[11] shoulders; and he walked heavily, dragging[12] his feet a little, the way a bear drags his paws[13]. His arms did not swing at his sides, but hung loosely[14].

The first man stopped short[15] in the clearing[16], and the follower nearly ran over him[17]. He took off his hat and wiped the sweat-band[18] with his forefinger and snapped the moisture[19] off. His huge companion dropped his blankets and flung himself down[20] and drank from the surface of the green pool; drank with long gulps, snorting[21] into the water like a horse. The small man stepped nervously beside him.

1. **stilted** guindé

2. **labored up into the air and pounded down river** se hissa dans les airs et survola lourdement la rivière

3. **in single file** en fil indienne

4. **brass** en cuivre

5. **shapeless** informes

6. **tight blanket rolls slung over** des couvertures roulées serrées jetées par-dessus
7. **with restless eyes** le regard vif
8. **features** traits
9. **slender arms** bras fins
10. **bony** osseux

11. **sloping** tombantes
12. **dragging** traînant
13. **paws** pattes

14. **hung loosely** pendaient, ballants
15. **short** net
16. **clearing** clairière
17. **ran over him** le renversa
18. **wiped the sweat-band** essuya le bandeau intérieur
19. **moisture** sueur
20. **flung himself down** se jeta au sol

21. **with long gulps, snorting** à grandes gorgées, s'ébrouant

"Lennie!" he said sharply[1]. "Lennie, for God' sakes[2] don't drink so much." Lennie continued to snort into the pool. The small man leaned over and shook him by the shoulder. "Lennie. You gonna[3] be sick like you was[4] last night."

Lennie dipped[5] his whole head under, hat and all, and then he sat up on the bank and his hat dripped down[6] on his blue coat and ran down his back. "Tha's[7] good," he said. "You drink some, George. You take a good big drink." He smiled happily.

George unslung his bindle[8] and dropped it gently on the bank. "I ain't[9] sure it's good water," he said. "Looks kinda scummy[10]."

Lennie dabbled[11] his big paw in the water and wiggled[12] his fingers so the water arose in little splashes; rings widened across the pool to the other side and came back again. Lennie watched them go. "Look, George. Look what I done[13]."

George knelt[14] beside the pool and drank from his hand with quick scoops[15]. "Tastes all right," he admitted. "Don't really seem to be running[16], though. You never oughtta[17] drink water when it ain't[18] running, Lennie," he said hopelessly. "You'd drink out of a gutter[19] if you was thirsty." He threw a scoop of water into his face and rubbed it[20] about with his hand, under his chin and around the back of his neck. Then he replaced his hat, pushed himself back from the river, drew up his knees[21] and embraced them. Lennie, who had been watching, imitated George exactly. He pushed himself back, drew up his knees, embraced them, looked over to George to see whether[1] he had it just right. He pulled his hat down a little more over his eyes, the way George's hat was.

George stared[2] morosely at the water. The rims[3] of his eyes were red with sun glare[4]. He said angrily, "We could just as well of rode clear[5] to the ranch if that bastard bus driver knew what he was talkin' about. 'Jes'[6] a little stretch[7] down the highway,' he says. 'Jes' a little stretch.' God damn near four miles, that's what it was! Didn't wanta[8] stop at the ranch gate, that's what. Too God damn lazy to pull up[9]. Wonder he isn't too damn good to stop in Soledad at all. Kicks us out and says, 'Jes' a little stretch down the road.' I bet it was more than four miles. Damn hot day."

Lennie looked timidly over to him. "George?"

"Yeah, what ya[10] want?"

"Where we goin'[11], George?"

The little man jerked down the brim of his hat and scowled over[12] at Lennie. "So you forgot that awready[13], did you? I gotta tell you again, do I? Jesus Christ, you're a crazy bastard!"

"I forgot," Lennie said softly. "I tried not to forget. Honest to God[14] I did, George."

"O.K.—O.K. I'll tell ya again. I ain't got nothing to do[15]. Might jus' as well spen'[16] all my time tellin'[17] you things and then you forget 'em[18], and I tell you again."

"Tried and tried," said Lennie, "but it didn't do no good. I remember about the rabbits, George."

1. **whether** si

2. **stared** fixait
3. **rims** bords
4. **sun glare** les rayons du soleil
5. **of rode clear** = have rode directly
6. **jes'** = just

7. **stretch** bout de route

8. **wanta** = want to

9. **pull up** = stop

10. **ya** = do you

11. **Where we goin'** = where are we going

12. **jerked down the brim of his hat and scowled over** inclina d'un coup sec le bord de son chapeau et jeta un regard noir
13. **awready** = already

14. **honest to God** je te jure
15. **I ain't got nothing to do** = I have nothing else to do
16. **spen'** = spend
17. **tellin'** = telling
18. **'em** = them

1. **the hell with** assez avec
2. **is them** = are those

3. **settin'** = sitting

4. **broke into a delighted smile** se fendit d'un sourire ravi
5. **what'd** = what did

6. **work cards** des cartes de travail

7. **gently** doucement
8. **musta** = must have

9. **grinned with relief** eut un grand sourire soulagé

10. **outta** = out of

11. **ain't** = there isn't
12. **cleverly** ingénieusement

13. **hidin'** = hiding

14. **give it here** donne moi ça

15. **on'y** = only

"The hell with[1] the rabbits. That's all you ever can remember is them[2] rabbits. O.K.! Now you listen and this time you got to remember so we don't get in no trouble. You remember settin'[3] in that gutter on Howard Street and watchin' that blackboard?"

Lennie's face broke into a delighted smile[4]. "Why sure, George, I remember that . . . but . . . what'd[5] we do then? I remember some girls come by and you says . . . you say . . ."

"The hell with what I says. You remember about us goin' into Murray and Ready's, and they give us work cards[6] and bus tickets?"

"Oh, sure, George. I remember that now." His hands went quickly into his side coat pockets. He said gently[7], "George . . . I ain't got mine. I musta[8] lost it." He looked down at the ground in despair.

"You never had none, you crazy bastard. I got both of 'em here. Think I'd let you carry your own work card?"

Lennie grinned with relief[9]. "I . . . I thought I put it in my side pocket." His hand went into the pocket again.

George looked sharply at him. "What'd you take outta[10] that pocket?"

"Ain't[11] a thing in my pocket," Lennie said cleverly[12].

"I know there ain't. You got it in your hand. What you got in your hand—hidin'[13] it?"

"I ain't got nothin', George. Honest."

"Come on, give it here[14]."

Lennie held his closed hand away from George's direction. "It's on'y[15] a mouse, George."

"A mouse? A live mouse[1]?"

"Uh-uh. Jus' a dead mouse, George. I didn' *kill* it. Honest! I found it. I found it dead."

"Give it here!" said George.

"Aw, leave me have it, George."

"Give it here!"

Lennie's closed hand slowly obeyed. George took the mouse and threw it across the pool to the other side, among the brush. "What you want of a dead mouse, anyways?"

"I could pet it with my thumb[2] while we walked along," said Lennie.

"Well, you ain't petting no mice[3] while you walk with me. You remember where we're goin'[4] now?"

Lennie looked startled[5] and then in embarrassment hid his face against his knees. "I forgot again."

"Jesus Christ," George said resignedly. "Well—look, we're gonna work on a ranch like the one we come from up north."

"Up north?"

"In Weed[6]."

"Oh, sure. I remember. In Weed."

"That ranch we're goin' to is right down there about a quarter mile. We're gonna go in an'[7] see the boss. Now, look—I'll give him the work tickets, but you ain't gonna say a word. You jus' stand there and don't say nothing. If he finds out what a crazy bastard you are, we won't get no job, but if he sees ya work before he hears ya talk, we're set[8]. Ya got that?"

"Sure, George. Sure I got

11

1. **a live mouse**
   une souris vivante

2. **pet *it* with my thumb**
   caresser avec mon pouce

3. **mice** = plural of *mouse*

4. **goin'** = going

5. **looked startled**
   eut l'air surpris

6. **Weed** = another city in California

7. **an'** = and

8. **we're set** on est bon

"O.K. Now when we go in to see the boss, what you gonna do?"

"I . . . I," Lennie thought. His face grew tight[1] with thought. "I . . . ain't gonna say nothin'. Jus' gonna stan'[2] there."

"Good boy. That's swell[3]. You say that over two, three times so you sure won't forget it."

Lennie droned to himself[4] softly, " 'I ain't gonna say nothin' . . . I ain't gonna say nothin' . . . I ain't gonna say nothin'."

"O.K.," said George. "An' you ain't gonna do no bad things like you done in Weed, neither."

Lennie looked puzzled[5]. "Like I done in Weed?"

"Oh, so ya forgot that too, did ya? Well, I ain't gonna remind ya, fear ya do it again[6]."

A light of understanding broke on[7] Lennie's face. "They run us outta[8] Weed," he exploded triumphantly.

"Run us out, hell," said George disgustedly. "We run. They was lookin'[9] for us, but they didn't catch us."

Lennie giggled[10] happily. "I didn't forget that, you bet."

George lay back[11] on the sand and crossed his hands under his head, and Lennie imitated him, raising his he... to see whether he were doing it right. "God, you're a lot ...uble," said George. "I could get along[12] so easy and so ...s I didn't have you on my tail[13]. I could live so easy ...rbe have a girl."

For a ...
hopefully, "Lennie lay quiet[14], and then he said ... work on a ranch, George."

"Awright[1]. You got that. But we're gonna sleep here because I got a reason."

The day was going fast[2] now. Only the tops of the Gabilan mountains flamed with the light of the sun that had gone from the valley. A water snake slipped[3] along on the pool, its head held up like a little periscope. The reeds[4] jerked slightly in the current. Far off toward the highway a man shouted something, and another man shouted back. The sycamore limbs rustled[5] under a little wind that died immediately.

"George—why ain't we goin' on to the ranch and get some supper? They got supper at the ranch."

George rolled on his side. "No reason at all for you. I like it here. Tomorra we're gonna go to work. I seen thrashin' machines[6] on the way down. That means we'll be bucking[7] grain bags, bustin' a gut[8]. Tonight I'm gonna lay right here and look up. I like it."

Lennie got up on his knees and looked down at George. "Ain't we gonna have no supper?"

"Sure we are, if you gather up[9] some dead willow sticks. I got three cans of beans in my bindle. You get a fire ready. I'll give you a match[10] when you get the sticks together. Then we'll heat the beans and have supper."

Lennie said, "I like beans with ketchup."

"Well, we ain't got no ketchup. You go get wood. An' don't you fool around. It'll be dark before long[11]."

Lennie lumbered to his feet[12] and disappeared in the brush. George lay where he was and whistled softly[13]

1. **awright** = all right

2. **was going fast** déclinait vite

3. **slipped** glissait

4. **reeds** roseaux

5. **rustled** bruissaient

6. **thrashin' machines** batteuses
7. **bucking** se trimbaler
8. **bustin' a gut** à s'en péter les boyaux

9. **gather up** vas chercher

10. **a match** une allumette

11. **before long** bientôt

12. **lumbered to his feet** se releva lourdement
13. **whistled softly** sifflota

13

1. **splashings**
   éclaboussures

2. **came crashing back**
   revint avec fracas

3. **gi'me** = give me

4. **made an elaborate pantomime of innocence** feignit l'innocence de manière élaborée
5. **you ain't puttin' nothing over** tu vas pas me la faire

6. **sock you** cogner

7. **reluctantly**
   à contrecœur

8. **lyin'** étalée

9. **outstretched**
   tendue

10. **drew back** recula

11. **snapped** claqua

to himself. There were sounds of splashings[1] down the river in the direction Lennie had taken. George stopped whistling and listened.

"Poor bastard," he said softly, and then went on whistling again.

In a moment Lennie came crashing back[2] through the brush. He carried one small willow stick in his hand. George sat up. "Awright," he said brusquely. "Gi'me[3] that mouse!"

But Lennie made an elaborate pantomime of innocence[4]. "What mouse, George? I ain't got no mouse."

George held out his hand. "Come on. Give it to me. You ain't puttin' nothing over[5]."

Lennie hesitated, backed away, looked wildly at the brush line as though he contemplated running for his freedom. George said coldly, "You gonna give me that mouse or do I have to sock you[6]?"

"Give you what, George?"

"You know God damn well what. I want that mouse."

Lennie reluctantly[7] reached into his pocket. His voice broke a little. "I don't know why I can't keep it. It ain't nobody's mouse. I didn't steal it. I found it lyin'[8] right beside the road."

George's hand remained outstretched[9] imperiously. Slowly, like a terrier who doesn't want to bring a ball to its master, Lennie approached, drew back[10], approached again. George snapped[11] his fingers sharply, and at the sound Lennie laid the mouse in his hand.

"I wasn't doin' nothing bad with it, George. Jus' strokin' it [1]."

George stood up and threw the mouse as far as he could into the darkening brush, and then he stepped to[2] the pool and washed his hands. "You crazy fool. Don't you think I could see your feet was wet[3] where you went acrost[4] the river to get it?" He heard Lennie's whimpering cry and wheeled about[5]. "Blubberin'[6] like a baby! Jesus Christ! A big guy like you." Lennie's lip quivered[7] and tears started in his eyes. "Aw, Lennie!" George put his hand on Lennie's shoulder. "I ain't takin' it away jus' for meanness[8]. That mouse ain't fresh, Lennie; and besides, you've broke it pettin' it. You get another mouse that's fresh and I'll let you keep it a little while."

Lennie sat down on the ground and hung his head dejectedly[9]. "I don't know where there is no other mouse. I remember a lady used to give 'em to me—ever'[10] one she got. But that lady ain't here."

George scoffed[11]. "Lady, huh? Don't even remember who that lady was. That was your own Aunt Clara. An' she stopped givin' 'em to ya. You always killed 'em."

Lennie looked sadly up at him. "They was[12] so little," he said, apologetically[13]. "I'd pet 'em, and pretty soon they bit my fingers and I pinched[14] their heads a little and then they was dead—because they was so little.

"I wisht[15] we'd get the rabbits pretty soon, George. They ain't so little."

1. **strokin' it** la caresser

2. **stepped to** s'approcha de
3. **wet** mouillés
4. **acrost** = across

5. **whimpering cry and wheeled about** pleurnichements et se retourna brusquement
6. **blubberin'** chialer
7. **quivered** trembla

8. **for meanness** pour être méchant

9. **dejectedly** d'un air abattu

10. **ever'** = every

11. **scoffed** se moqua

12. **they was** = they were

13. **apologetically** d'un air désolé
14. **pinched** pinçais

15. **wisht** = wish

1. **rubber** en caoutchouc

2. **lifted** se souleva

3. **dusk** crépuscule

4. **gulped air** prit une goulée d'air
5. **sank** s'enfonça
6. **widening** de plus en plus larges
7. **overhead** au-dessus d'eux
8. **whisked** frémirent
9. **puffs** touffes

10. **floodwater wood** du bois venu avec la crue

11. **a litter** tout un tas
12. **twigs** des brindilles
13. **in a heap** en une pile
14. **dove** colombe

15. **undid his bindle** défit son baluchon

16. **blaze** brasier

"The hell with the rabbits. An' you ain't to be trusted with no live mice. Your Aunt Clara give you a rubber[1] mouse and you wouldn't have nothing to do with it."

"It wasn't no good to pet," said Lennie.

The flame of the sunset lifted[2] from the mountaintops and dusk[3] came into the valley, and a half darkness came in among the willows and the sycamores. A big carp rose to the surface of the pool, gulped air[4] and then sank[5] mysteriously into the dark water again, leaving widening[6] rings on the water. Overhead[7] the leaves whisked[8] again and little puffs[9] of willow cotton blew down and landed on the pool's surface.

"You gonna get that wood?" George demanded. "There's plenty right up against the back of that sycamore. Floodwater wood[10]. Now you get it."

Lennie went behind the tree and brought out a litter[11] of dried leaves and twigs[12]. He threw them in a heap[13] on the old ash pile and went back for more and more. It was almost night now. A dove's[14] wings whistled over the water. George walked to the fire pile and lighted the dry leaves. The flame cracked up among the twigs and fell to work. George undid his bindle[15] and brought out three cans of beans. He stood them about the fire, close in against the blaze[16], but not quite touching the flame.

"There's enough beans for four men," George said.

Lennie watched him from over the fire. He said patiently, "I like 'em with ketchup."

"Well, we ain't got any," George exploded. "Whatever we ain't got, that's what you want. God a'mighty[1], if I was alone I could live so easy. I could go get a job an' work, an' no trouble. No mess[2] at all, and when the end of the month come I could take my fifty bucks[3] and go into town and get whatever I want. Why,[4] I could stay in a cat house[5] all night. I could eat any place I want, hotel or any place, and order any damn thing I could think of. An' I could do all that every damn month. Get a gallon[6] of whisky, or set in a poolroom[7] and play cards or shoot pool." Lennie knelt[8] and looked over the fire at the angry George. And Lennie's face was drawn with terror.

"An' whatta I got[9]," George went on furiously. "I got you! You can't keep a job and you lose me ever' job I get. Jus' keep me shovin'[10] all over the country all the time. An' that ain't the worst. You get in trouble. You do bad things and I got to get you out." His voice rose nearly to a shout. "You crazy son-of-a-bitch. You keep me in hot water[11] all the time." He took on the elaborate manner of little girls when they are mimicking[12] one another. "Jus' wanted to feel that girl's dress—jus' wanted to pet it like it was a mouse— Well, how the hell did she know you jus' wanted to feel her dress? She jerks back and you hold on like it was a mouse. She yells[13] and we got to hide in a irrigation ditch[14] all day with guys lookin' for us, and we got to sneak out[15] in the dark and get outta the country. All the time somethin' like that—all the time. I wisht I could put

1. **God a'mighty** = God almighty = bon Dieu
2. **mess** problème
3. **bucks** = dollars
4. **why,** eh, même que
5. **cat house** maison close
6. **1 gallon** = 3,7 litres
7. **poolroom** salle de billard
8. **knelt** s'agenouilla
9. **an' whatta I got** = and what have I got
10. **shovin'** balader
11. **hot water** = trouble
12. **are mimicking** imitent
13. **yells** hurle
14. **ditch** fossé
15. **sneak out** se faire la malle

you in a cage with about a million mice an' let you have fun." His anger left him suddenly. He looked across the fire at Lennie's anguished face, and then he looked ashamedly[1] at the flames.

It was quite dark now, but the fire lighted the trunks[2] of the trees and the curving branches overhead. Lennie crawled slowly and cautiously[3] around the fire until he was close to George. He sat back on his heels. George turned the bean cans so that another side faced the fire. He pretended to be unaware[4] of Lennie so close beside him.

"George," very softly. No answer. "George!"

"Whatta[5] you want?"

"I was only foolin'[6], George. I don't want no ketchup. I wouldn't eat no ketchup if it was right here beside me."

"If it was here, you could have some."

"But I wouldn't eat none, George. I'd leave it all for you. You could cover your beans with it and I wouldn't touch none of it."

George still stared morosely[7] at the fire. "When I think of the swell time I could have without you, I go nuts[8]. I never get no peace."

Lennie still knelt. He looked off into the darkness across the river. "George, you want I should go away and leave you alone?"

"Where the hell could you go?"

"Well, I could. I could go off in the hills there. Someplace I'd find a cave[9]."

1. **ashamedly** honteusement
2. **trunks** troncs
3. **crawled slowly and cautiously** s'approcha doucement et prudemment à quatre pattes
4. **to be unaware** ne pas se rendre compte
5. **whatta** = what do
6. **foolin'** = joking
7. **morosely** sombrement
8. **nuts** = crazy
9. **cave** grotte

"Yeah? How'd you eat. You ain't got sense[1] enough to find nothing to eat."

"I'd find things, George. I don't need no nice food with ketchup. I'd lay out in the sun and nobody'd hurt me. An' if I foun' a mouse, I could keep it. Nobody'd[2] take it away from me."

George looked quickly and searchingly[3] at him. "I been mean, ain't I?"

"If you don' want me I can go off in the hills an' find a cave. I can go away any time."

"No—look! I was jus' foolin', Lennie. 'Cause[4] I want you to stay with me. Trouble with mice is you always kill 'em." He paused. "Tell you what I'll do, Lennie. First chance I get I'll give you a pup[5]. Maybe you wouldn't kill it. That'd be better than mice. And you could pet it harder."

Lennie avoided the bait[6]. He had sensed his advantage. "If you don't want me, you only jus' got to say so, and I'll go off in those hills right there—right up in those hills and live by myself. An' I won't get no mice stole[7] from me."

George said, "I want you to stay with me, Lennie. Jesus Christ, somebody'd shoot you for a coyote if you was by yourself. No, you stay with me. Your Aunt Clara wouldn't like you running off by yourself, even if she is dead."

Lennie spoke craftily[8], "Tell me—like you done before."

"Tell you what?"

1. sense jugeote

2. nobody'd = nobody would

3. searchingly avec curiosité

4. 'cause = because

5. pup chiot

6. avoided the bait ne mordit pas à l'hameçon

7. stole = stolen

8. craftily astucieusement

19

"About the rabbits."

George snapped[1], "You ain't gonna put nothing over on me[2]."

Lennie pleaded[3], "Come on, George. Tell me. Please George. Like you done before."

"You get a kick[4] outta that, don't you? Awright, I'll tell you, and then we'll eat our supper…"

George's voice became deeper. He repeated his words rhythmically as though[5] he had said them many times before. "Guys like us, that work on ranches, are the loneliest[6] guys in the world. They got no family. They don't belong no place. They come to a ranch an' work up a stake[7] and then they go inta[8] town and blow their stake[9], and the first thing you know they're poundin' their tail[10] on some other ranch. They ain't got nothing to look ahead to."

Lennie was delighted[11]. "That's it—that's it. Now tell how it is with us."

George went on. "With us it ain't like that. We got a future. We got somebody to talk to that gives a damn[12] about us. We don't have to sit in no bar room blowin' in our jack[13] jus' because we got no place else to go. If them other guys gets in jail they can rot[14] for all anybody gives a damn. But not us."

Lennie broke in[15]. "But not us! An' why? Because . . . because I got you to look after[16] me, and you got me to look after you, and that's why." He laughed delightedly. "Go on now, George!"

"You got it by heart. You can do it yourself."

---

1. **snapped** éclata

2. **you ain't gonna put nothing over on me** faut pas me la faire, à moi
3. **pleaded** implora

4. **get a kick** prends ton pied

5. **as though** = as if

6. **the loneliest** les plus solitaires

7. **work up a stake** = make some money
8. **inta** = into
9. **blow their stake** = spend all their money
10. **poundin' their tail** s'échinent

11. **delighted** aux anges

12. **that gives a damn** qui en a quelque chose à faire

13. **blowin' in our jack** = wasting our money
14. **rot** pourrir

15. **broke in** le coupa

16. **look after** t'occuper de

"No, you. I forget some a'[1] the things. Tell about how it's gonna be."

"O.K. Someday—we're gonna get the jack together and we're gonna have a little house and a couple of acres[2] an' a cow and some pigs and——"

"*An' live off the fatta the lan'*[3]," Lennie shouted. "An' have *rabbits*. Go on, George! Tell about what we're gonna have in the garden and about the rabbits in the cages and about the rain in the winter and the stove[4], and how thick the cream is on the milk like you can hardly[5] cut it. Tell about that, George."

"Why'n't[6] you do it yourself? You know all of it."

"No . . . you tell it. It ain't the same if I tell it. Go on . . . George. How I get to tend[7] the rabbits."

"Well," said George, "we'll have a big vegetable patch and a rabbit hutch[8] and chickens. And when it rains in the winter, we'll just say the hell with goin' to work, and we'll build up a fire[9] in the stove and set around it an' listen to the rain comin' down on the roof—Nuts![10]" He took out his pocket knife. "I ain't got time for no more." He drove his knife through the top of one of the bean cans, sawed out[11] the top and passed the can to Lennie. Then he opened a second can. From his side pocket he brought out two spoons and passed one of them to Lennie.

They sat by the fire and filled their mouths with beans and chewed mightily[12]. A few beans slipped out of the side of Lennie's mouth. George gestured with his spoon. "What you gonna say tomorrow when the boss asks you questions?"

1. **some a'** = some of
2. **2 acres** = 1 hectare
3. **live off the fatta the lan'** = live off the fat of the land = vivre comme des rentiers
4. **stove** poêle
5. **hardly** à peine
6. **why'n't** = why don't you
7. **tend** m'occuper de
8. **a vegetable patch and a rabbit hutch** un potager et un clapier à lapins
9. **we'll build up a fire** on fera un feu
10. **nuts!** zut !
11. **sawed out** découpa
12. **chewed mightily** mastiquèrent vigoureusement

Lennie stopped chewing and swallowed[1]. His face was concentrated. "I… I ain't gonna… say a word."

"Good boy! That's fine[2], Lennie! Maybe you're gettin' better. When we get the coupla[3] acres I can let you tend the rabbits all right. 'Specially if you remember as good as that."

Lennie choked with pride[4]. "I can remember," he said.

George motioned[5] with his spoon again. "Look, Lennie. I want you to look around here. You can remember this place, can't you? The ranch is about a quarter mile up[6] that way. Just follow the river."

"Sure," said Lennie. "I can remember this. Di'n't[7] I remember about not gonna say a word?"

"'Course[8] you did. Well, look. Lennie—if you jus' happen to get in trouble[9] like you always done before, I want you to come right here an' hide in the brush."

"Hide in the brush," said Lennie slowly.

"Hide in the brush till I come for you. Can you remember that?"

"Sure I can, George. Hide in the brush till you come."

"But you ain't gonna get in no trouble, because if you do, I won't let you tend the rabbits." He threw his empty bean can off into the brush.

"I won't get in no trouble, George. I ain't gonna say a word."

"O.K. Bring your bindle over here by the fire. It's gonna be nice sleepin' here. Lookin' up, and the leaves. Don't build up no more fire. We'll let her die down[10]."

1. swallowed avala

2. that's fine = that's great
3. coupla = couple of

4. choked with pride s'étouffa d'orgueil

5. motioned fit un geste

6. a quarter mile up à 400 mètres
7. di'n't = didn't

8. 'course = of course

9. if you jus' happen to get in trouble si par hasard tu te fous dans le pétrin

10. die down s'éteindre

They made their beds on the sand, and as the blaze dropped from the fire the sphere of light grew smaller; the curling[1] branches disappeared and only a faint glimmer[2] showed where the tree trunks were. From the darkness Lennie called, "George—you asleep?"

"No. Whatta you want?"

"Let's have different color rabbits, George."

"Sure we will," George said sleepily. "Red and blue and green rabbits, Lennie. Millions of 'em."

"Furry ones[3], George, like I seen in the fair[4] in Sacramento."

"Sure, furry ones."

"'Cause I can jus' as well go away, George, an' live in a cave."

"You can jus' as well go to hell," said George. "Shut up now."

The red light dimmed on the coals[5]. Up the hill from the river a coyote yammered[6], and a dog answered from the other side of the stream. The sycamore leaves whispered[7] in a little night breeze.

1. **curling** sinueuses

2. **faint glimmer** faible lueur

3. **furry ones** avec des poils longs
4. **fair** foire

5. **dimmed on the coals** faiblit sur les braises
6. **yammered** brailla

7. **whispered** murmurèrent

II

PREVIOUSLY ON...

résumé
des épisodes
précédents

The bunk house[1] was a long, rectangular building. Inside, the walls were whitewashed[2] and the floor unpainted. In three walls there were small, square windows, and in the fourth, a solid door with a wooden latch[3]. Against the walls were eight bunks[4], five of them made up with blankets and the other three showing their burlap ticking[5]. Over each bunk there was nailed[6] an apple box with the opening forward so that it made two shelves[7] for the personal belongings of the occupant of the bunk. And these shelves were loaded with[8] little articles, soap and talcum powder, razors and those Western magazines ranch men love to read and scoff at[9] and secretly believe. And there were medicines on the shelves, and little vials, combs[10]; and from nails on the box sides, a few neckties[11]. Near one wall there was a black cast-iron[12] stove, its stovepipe[13] going straight up through the ceiling. In the middle of the room stood a big square table littered with[14] playing cards, and around it were grouped boxes for the players to sit on.

At about ten o'clock in the morning the sun threw a bright dust-laden bar[15] through one of the side windows, and in and out of the beam[16] flies shot[17] like rushing stars.

The wooden latch raised. The door opened and a tall, stoop-shouldered[18] old man came in. He was dressed in blue jeans and he carried a big push-broom[19] in his left hand. Behind him came George, and behind George, Lennie.

"The boss was expectin' you[1] last night," the old man said. "He was sore[2] as hell when you wasn't here to go out this morning." He pointed with his right arm, and out of the sleeve[3] came a round stick-like wrist[4], but no hand. "You can have them two beds there," he said, indicating two bunks near the stove.

George stepped over and threw his blankets down on the burlap sack of straw that was a mattress. He looked into his box shelf and then picked a small yellow can from it. "Say. What the hell's this?"

"I don't know," said the old man.

"Says 'positively kills lice, roaches and other scourges[5].' What the hell kind of bed you giving us, anyways? We don't want no pants rabbits[6]."

The old swamper[7] shifted his broom and held it between his elbow and his side while he held out his hand for the can. He studied the label[8] carefully. "Tell you what—" he said finally, "last guy that had this bed was a blacksmith[9]—hell of a nice fella[10] and as clean a guy as you want to meet. Used to wash his hands even *after* he ate."

"Then how come he got graybacks[11]?" George was working up a slow anger. Lennie put his bindle on the neighboring[12] bunk and sat down. He watched George with open mouth.

"Tell you what," said the old swamper. "This here blacksmith—name of Whitey—was the kind of guy that would put that stuff around even if there wasn't no bugs—just to make sure, see? Tell you what he used

1. **was expectin' you** vous attendait
2. **sore** remonté

3. **sleeve** manche
4. **stick-like wrist** poignet comme un bâton

5. **lice, roaches and other scourges** poux, cafards et autres vermines
6. **pants rabbits** morpions
7. **swamper** homme à tout faire
8. **label** étiquette

9. **blacksmith** forgeron
10. **nice fella** brave gars

11. **got graybacks** avait des morpions

12. **neighboring** d'à côté

1. **he'd peel his boil'
   potatoes** il épluchait
   ses patates bouillies
2. **splotch** tâche
3. **he'd scrape it off** il
   la raclait
4. **about** = because of
5. **dress up** se mettre
   sur son 31

6. **set** = sat

7. **bristly white
   whiskers with his
   knuckles** barbe
   blanche et rêche avec
   son poing

8. **gimme my time**
   donnez-moi ce qui
   m'est dû

9. **tick** matelas

10. **sacking** toile

11. **his liniment and
    leather wristband** sa
    pommade et son
    bracelet de cuir
12. **burned** en rogne

13. **give the stable buck
    hell** maltraite le garçon
    d'écurie
14. **patted a wrinkle out**
    effaça un pli

to do—At meals he'd peel his boil' potatoes[1], an' he'd take out ever' little spot, no matter what kind, before he'd eat it. And if there was a red splotch[2] on an egg, he'd scrape it off[3]. Finally quit about[4] the food. That's the kinda guy he was—clean. Used ta dress up[5] Sundays even when he wasn't going no place, put on a necktie even, and then set[6] in the bunk house."

"I ain't so sure," said George skeptically. "What did you say he quit for?"

The old man put the yellow can in his pocket, and he rubbed his bristly white whiskers with his knuckles[7]. "Why . . . he . . . just quit, the way a guy will. Says it was the food. Just wanted to move. Didn't give no other reason but the food. Just says 'gimme my time[8]' one night, the way any guy would."

George lifted his tick[9] and looked underneath it. He leaned over and inspected the sacking[10] closely. Immediately Lennie got up and did the same with his bed. Finally George seemed satisfied. He unrolled his bindle and put things on the shelf, his razor and bar of soap, his comb and bottle of pills, his liniment and leather wristband[11]. Then he made his bed up neatly with blankets. The old man said, "I guess the boss'll be out here in a minute. He was sure burned[12] when you wasn't here this morning. Come right in when we was eatin' breakfast and says, 'Where the hell's them new men?' An' he give the stable buck hell[13], too."

George patted a wrinkle out[14] of his bed, and sat down. "Give the stable buck hell?" he asked.

"Sure. Ya see the stable buck's a nigger[1]."

"Nigger, huh?"

"Yeah. Nice fella too. Got a crooked back[2] where a horse kicked him. The boss gives him hell when he's mad. But the stable buck don't give a damn about that. He reads a lot. Got books in his room."

"What kind of a guy is the boss?" George asked.

"Well, he's a pretty nice fella. Gets pretty mad sometimes, but he's pretty nice. Tell ya what—know what he done[3] Christmas? Brang[4] a gallon of whisky right in here and says, 'Drink hearty[5] boys. Christmas comes but once a year.' "

"The hell he did! Whole gallon?"

"Yes sir. Jesus, we had fun. They let the nigger come in that night. Little skinner[6] name of Smitty took after[7] the nigger. Done pretty good, too. The guys wouldn't let him use his feet, so the nigger got him[8]. If he coulda[9] used his feet, Smitty says he woulda killed the nigger. The guys said on account of[10] the nigger's got a crooked back, Smitty can't use his feet." He paused in relish of[11] the memory. "After that the guys went into Soledad and raised hell[12]. I didn't go in there. I ain't got the poop no more.[13]"

Lennie was just finishing making his bed. The wooden latch raised again and the door opened. A little stocky[14] man stood in the open doorway. He wore blue jean trousers, a flannel shirt, a black, unbuttoned vest and a black coat. His thumbs were stuck in his belt, on each side of a square steel buckle[15]. On

1. **nigger** = negro (discriminatory racial slur)

2. **crooked back** dos pas droit

3. **he done** = he did for
4. **brang** = brought
5. **drink hearty** buvez tout votre saoul

6. **skinner** muletier
7. **took after** = started a fight with

8. **got him** = won
9. **coulda** = could have

10. **on account of** = because
11. **in relish of** savourant

12. **raised hell** ont fait la bringue
13. **I ain't got the poop no more** j'ai plus l'énergie

14. **stocky** trapu

15. **square steel buckle** boucle de ceinture carrée en acier

29

his head was a soiled brown Stetson hat[1], and he wore high-heeled boots and spurs[2] to prove he was not a laboring man[3].

The old swamper looked quickly at him, and then shuffled[4] to the door rubbing his whiskers with his knuckles as he went. "Them guys just come," he said, and shuffled past the boss and out the door.

The boss stepped into the room with the short, quick steps of a fat-legged man. "I wrote Murray and Ready I wanted two men this morning. You got your work slips[5]?" George reached into his pocket and produced the slips and handed them to the boss. "It wasn't Murray and Ready's fault. Says right here on the slip that you was to be here for work this morning."

George looked down at his feet. "Bus driver give us a bum steer[6]," he said. "We hadda[7] walk ten miles. Says we was here when we wasn't. We couldn't get no rides[8] in the morning."

The boss squinted[9] his eyes. "Well, I had to send out the grain teams short two buckers[10]. Won't do any good to go out now till after dinner[11]." He pulled his time book out of his pocket and opened it where a pencil was stuck between the leaves. George scowled meaningfully[12] at Lennie, and Lennie nodded[13] to show that he understood. The boss licked his pencil. "What's your name?"

"George Milton."

"And what's yours?"

George said, "His name's Lennie Small."

The names were entered in the book. "Le's¹ see, this is the twentieth, noon the twentieth." He closed the book. "Where you boys been working?"

"Up around Weed," said George. "You, too?" to Lennie.

"Yeah, him too," said George.

The boss pointed a playful finger at Lennie. "He ain't much of a talker², is he?"

"No, he ain't, but he's sure a hell of a good worker. Strong as a bull³."

Lennie smiled to himself. "Strong as a bull," he repeated.

George scowled at him, and Lennie dropped his head in shame at having forgotten.

The boss said suddenly, "Listen, Small!" Lennie raised his head. "What can you do?"

In a panic, Lennie looked at George for help. "He can do anything you tell him," said George. "He's a good skinner. He can rassle⁴ grain bags, drive a cultivator. He can do anything. Just give him a try."

The boss turned on George. "Then why don't you let him answer? What you trying to put over?⁵"

George broke in loudly, "Oh! I ain't saying he's bright⁶. He ain't. But I say he's a God damn good worker. He can put up a four hundred pound bale⁷."

The boss deliberately put the little book in his pocket. He hooked his thumbs in his belt and squinted one eye nearly closed. "Say—what you sellin'⁸?"

"Huh?"

1. le's = let's
2. he ain't much of a talker c'est pas un bavard
3. bull taureau
4. rassle porter
5. what you trying to put over? qu'est ce que t'as derrière la tête ?
6. bright futé
7. a four hundred pound bale une charge de 180 kilos
8. sellin' = selling

31

"I said what stake you got[1] in this guy? You takin' his pay away from him?"

"No, 'course I ain't. Why ya think I'm sellin' him out?"

"Well, I never seen one guy take so much trouble for another guy. I just like to know what your interest is."

George said, "He's my . . . cousin. I told his old lady I'd take care of him[2]. He got kicked in the head by a horse when he was a kid. He's awright. Just ain't bright. But he can do anything you tell him."

The boss turned half away. "Well, God knows he don't need any brains to buck barley bags[3]. But don't you try to put nothing over[4], Milton. I got my eye on you. Why'd you quit in Weed?"

"Job was done," said George promptly.

"What kinda job?"

"We . . . we was diggin' a cesspool[5]."

"All right. But don't try to put nothing over, 'cause you can't get away with nothing[6]. I seen wise guys[7] before. Go on out with the grain teams after dinner. They're pickin' up barley at the threshing machine[8]. Go out with Slim's team."

"Slim?"

"Yeah. Big tall skinner. You'll see him at dinner." He turned abruptly and went to the door, but before he went out he turned and looked for a long moment at the two men.

When the sound of his footsteps had died away, George turned on Lennie. "So you wasn't gonna say

2. I'd take care of him
   que je m'occuperais de
   lui

3. buck barley bags
   porter des sacs d'orge
4. don't you try to put
   nothing over essaye
   pas de me la faire

5. diggin' a cesspool
   creusait une fosse
   septique

6. you can't get away
   with nothing tu pourras
   pas t'en sortir comme ça
7. wise guys des malins
8. threshing machine
   batteuses

a word. You was gonna leave your big flapper[1] shut and leave me do the talkin'. Damn near lost us the job."

Lennie stared hopelessly at his hands. "I forgot, George."

"Yeah, you forgot. You always forget, an' I got to talk you out of it[2]." He sat down heavily on the bunk. "Now he's got his eye on us. Now we got to be careful and not make no slips[3]. You keep your big flapper shut after this." He fell morosely silent.

"George."

"What you want now?"

"I wasn't kicked in the head with no horse, was I, George?"

"Be a damn good thing if you was," George said viciously[4]. "Save ever'body a hell of a lot of trouble."

"You said I was your cousin, George."

"Well, that was a lie. An' I'm damn glad it was. If I was a relative of yours[5] I'd shoot myself." He stopped suddenly, stepped to the open front door and peered out[6]. "Say, what the hell you doin' listenin'?"

The old man came slowly into the room. He had his broom in his hand. And at his heels there walked a dragfooted sheep dog[7], gray of muzzle[8], and with pale, blind old eyes. The dog struggled lamely[9] to the side of the room and lay down, grunting[10] softly to himself and licking his grizzled, moth-eaten coat[11]. The swamper watched him until he was settled[12]. "I wasn't listenin'. I was jus' standin' in the shade a minute scratchin'

1. **flapper** clapet

2. **I got to talk you out of it** je dois te sortir de là

3. **slips** bourdes

4. **viciously** méchamment

5. **a relative of yours** de ta famille

6. **peered out** jeta un coup d'œil dehors

7. **dragfooted sheep dog** chien de berger aux pattes traînantes
8. **muzzle** museau
9. **struggled lamely** boita péniblement
10. **grunting** grognant
11. **grizzled, moth-eaten coat** pelage gris et miteux
12. **settled** installé

1. **swampin'** balayer

2. **pokin'** fourrer
3. **get nosey** fouiner
4. **uneasily** gêné

5. **ast** = ask

6. **mollified** calmé

7. **set down** pose-toi

8. **bristled cheek** joue
   barbue

9. **tightly curled** crépus

10. **my old man** mon père

my dog. I jus' now finished swampin'[1] out the wash house."

"You was pokin'[2] your big ears into our business," George said. "I don't like nobody to get nosey[3]."

The old man looked uneasily[4] from George to Lennie, and then back. "I jus' come there," he said. "I didn't hear nothing you guys was sayin'. I ain't interested in nothing you was sayin'. A guy on a ranch don't never listen nor he don't ast[5] no questions."

"Damn right he don't," said George, slightly mollified[6], "not if he wants to stay workin' long." But he was reassured by the swamper's defense. "Come on in and set down[7] a minute," he said. "That's a hell of an old dog."

"Yeah. I had 'im ever since he was a pup. God, he was a good sheep dog when he was younger." He stood his broom against the wall and he rubbed his white bristled cheek[8] with his knuckles. "How'd you like the boss?" he asked.

"Pretty good. Seemed awright."

"He's a nice fella," the swamper agreed. "You got to take him right."

At that moment a young man came into the bunk house; a thin young man with a brown face, with brown eyes and a head of tightly curled[9] hair. He wore a work glove on his left hand, and, like the boss, he wore high-heeled boots. "Seen my old man[10]?" he asked.

The swamper said, "He was here jus' a minute ago, Curley. Went over to the cook house, I think."

"I'll try to catch him," said Curley. His eyes passed over the new men and he stopped. He glanced[1] coldly at George and then at Lennie. His arms gradually bent[2] at the elbows and his hands closed into fists. He stiffened[3] and went into a slight crouch[4]. His glance was at once calculating and pugnacious[5]. Lennie squirmed[6] under the look and shifted his feet nervously. Curley stepped gingerly[7] close to him. "You the new guys the old man was waitin' for?"

"We just come in," said George.

"Let the big guy talk."

Lennie twisted with embarrassment.

George said, "S'pose[8] he don't want to talk?"

Curley lashed his body around[9]. "By Christ, he's gotta talk when he's spoke[10] to. What the hell are you gettin' into it for?"

"We travel together," said George coldly.

"Oh, so it's that way."

George was tense, and motionless[11]. "Yeah, it's that way."

Lennie was looking helplessly to George for instruction.

"An' you won't let the big guy talk, is that it?" "He can talk if he wants to tell you anything." He nodded slightly[12] to Lennie.

"We jus' come in," said Lennie softly.

Curley stared levelly[13] at him. "Well, nex' time you answer when you're spoke to." He turned toward the door and walked out, and his elbows were still bent out a little.

1. **glanced** jeta un coup d'œil
2. **bent** plièrent
3. **stiffened** se raidit
4. **went into a slight crouch** se baissa légèrement
5. **pugnacious** agressif
6. **squirmed** se tortilla
7. **gingerly** avec précaution
8. **s'pose** = suppose = what if
9. **lashed his body around** se retourna d'un coup
10. **spoke** = spoken
11. **motionless** immobile
12. **nodded slightly** fit un petit signe de tête
13. **levelly** fixement

George watched him out, and then he turned back to the swamper. "Say, what the hell's he got on his shoulder[1]? Lennie didn't do nothing to him."

The old man looked cautiously at the door to make sure no one was listening. "That's the boss's son," he said quietly. "Curley's pretty handy[2]. He done quite a bit in the ring. He's a lightweight[3], and he's handy."

"Well, let him be handy," said George. "He don't have to take after[4] Lennie. Lennie didn't do nothing to him. What's he got against Lennie?"

The swamper considered. . . "Well . . . tell you what. Curley's like a lot of little guys. He hates big guys. He's alla time picking scraps[5] with big guys. Kind of like he's mad at 'em because he ain't a big guy. You seen little guys like that, ain't you? Always scrappy[6]?"

"Sure," said George. "I seen plenty tough little guys[7]. But this Curley better not make no mistakes about Lennie. Lennie ain't handy, but this Curley punk[8] is gonna get hurt if he messes around with[9] Lennie."

"Well, Curley's pretty handy," the swamper said skeptically. "Never did seem right to me. S'pose Curley jumps[10] a big guy an' licks him[11]. Ever'body says what a game guy[12] Curley is. And s'pose he does the same thing and gets licked. Then ever'body says the big guy oughtta[13] pick on somebody his own size, and maybe they gang up on[14] the big guy. Never did seem right to me. Seems like Curley ain't givin' nobody a chance."

---

1. **what the hell's he got on his shoulder** pourquoi il s'énerve comme ça celui-là ?

2. **handy** habile

3. **lightweight** poids léger (boxe)

4. **take after** venir embêter

5. **alla time picking scraps** cherche toujours des noises

6. **scrappy** énervés

7. **tough little guys** des petits durs

8. **punk** minable

9. **messes around with** embête

10. **jumps** s'attaque à
11. **licks him** lui fout une raclée
12. **a game guy** un type qui sait y faire

13. **oughtta** = ought to

14. **gang up on** se liguent contre

George was watching the door. He said ominously[1], "Well, he better watch out for Lennie. Lennie ain't no fighter, but Lennie's strong and quick and Lennie don't know no rules." He walked to the square table and sat down on one of the boxes. He gathered[2] some of the cards together and shuffled[3] them.

The old man sat down on another box. "Don't tell Curley I said none of this. He'd slough me[4]. He just don't give a damn. Won't ever get canned[5] 'cause his old man's the boss."

George cut the cards and began turning them over, looking at each one and throwing it down on a pile. He said, "This guy Curley sounds like a son-of-a-bitch to me. I don't like mean little guys."

"Seems to me like he's worse lately," said the swamper. "He got married a couple of weeks ago. Wife lives over in the boss's house. Seems like Curley is cockier'n ever[6] since he got married."

George grunted, "Maybe he's showin' off[7] for his wife."

The swamper warmed to his gossip. "You seen that glove on his left hand?"

"Yeah. I seen it."

"Well, that glove's fulla[8] Vaseline."

"Vaseline? What the hell for?"

"Well, I tell ya what—Curley says he's keepin' that hand soft for his wife."

George studied the cards absorbedly. "That's a dirty thing to tell around," he said.

---

1. **ominously** d'un ton menaçant
2. **gathered... together** ramassa
3. **shuffled** mélangea
4. **he'd slough me** il me jetterait dehors
5. **canned** renvoyé
6. **cockier'n ever** plus prétentieux que jamais
7. **he's showin' off** il frime
8. **fulla** = full of

The old man was reassured. He had drawn a derogatory statement[1] from George. He felt safe now, and he spoke more confidently. "Wait'll[2] you see Curley's wife."

George cut the cards again and put out a solitaire[3] lay, slowly and deliberately. "Purty[4]?" he asked casually.

"Yeah. Purty . . . but——"

George studied his cards. "But what?"

"Well—she got the eye[5]."

"Yeah? Married two weeks and got the eye? Maybe that's why Curley's pants is full of ants[6]."

"I seen her give Slim the eye. Slim's a jerkline skinner[7]. Hell of a nice fella. Slim don't need to wear no high-heeled boots on a grain team. I seen her give Slim the eye. Curley never seen it. An' I seen her give Carlson the eye."

George pretended a lack of interest. "Looks like we was gonna have fun."

The swamper stood up from his box. "Know what I think?" George did not answer. "Well, I think Curley's married . . . a tart[8]."

"He ain't the first," said George. "There's plenty done that."

The old man moved toward the door, and his ancient[9] dog lifted his head and peered about, and then got painfully to his feet to follow. "I gotta be settin' out the wash basins for the guys. The teams'll be in before long[10]. You guys gonna buck barley?"

"Yeah."

"You won't tell Curley nothing I said?"

---

1. **drawn a derogatory statement** tiré un commentaire péjoratif
2. **wait'll** = wait until
3. **a solitaire** une réussite
4. **purty** = pretty
5. **she got the eye** elle fait de l'œil
6. **Curley's pants is full of ants** il est sur les nerfs
7. **a jerkline skinner** celui qui conduit les mules
8. **a tart** une chaudasse
9. **ancient** = very old
10. **before long** = soon

"Hell no."

"Well, you look her over[1], mister. You see if she ain't a tart." He stepped out the door into the brilliant sunshine.

George laid down his cards thoughtfully[2], turned his piles of three. He built four clubs on his ace pile[3]. The sun square was on the floor now, and the flies whipped through it like sparks[4]. A sound of jingling harness and the croak of heavy-laden axles[5] sounded from outside. From the distance came a clear call. "Stable Buck— ooh, sta-able Buck!" And then, "Where the hell is that God damn nigger?"

George stared at[6] his solitaire lay, and then he flounced[7] the cards together and turned around to Lennie. Lennie was lying down on the bunk watching him.

"Look, Lennie! This here ain't no setup[8]. I'm scared. You gonna have trouble with that Curley guy. I seen that kind before. He was kinda feelin' you out[9]. He figures[10] he's got you scared and he's gonna take a sock[11] at you the first chance he gets."

Lennie's eyes were frightened. "I don't want no trouble," he said plaintively. "Don't let him sock me, George."

George got up and went over to Lennie's bunk and sat down on it. "I hate that kinda bastard," he said. "I seen plenty[12] of 'em. Like the old guy says, Curley don't take no chances. He always wins." He thought for a moment. "If he tangles[13] with you, Lennie, we're gonna get the can[14]. Don't make no mistake about that. He's

1. **you look her over** jettes-y un coup d'œil

2. **thoughtfully** pensivement
3. **built four clubs on his ace pile** mit quatre trèfles sur sa pile d'as

4. **sparks** étincelles

5. **the croak of heavy-laden axles** le grincement des roues d'une charrette bien chargée

6. **stared at** fixa
7. **flounced** mélangea

8. **no setup** pas une blague

9. **was feelin' you out** te jaugeait
10. **figures** pense
11. **a sock** une raclée

12. **plenty** beaucoup

13. **tangles** = fights, argues
14. **get the can** être virés

the boss's son. Look, Lennie. You try to keep away from him, will you? Don't never speak to him. If he comes in here you move clear[1] to the other side of the room. Will you do that, Lennie?"

"I don't want no trouble," Lennie mourned[2]. "I never done nothing to him."

"Well, that won't do you no good if Curley wants to plug himself up[3] for a fighter. Just don't have nothing to do with him. Will you remember?"

"Sure, George. I ain't gonna say a word."

The sound of the approaching grain teams was louder, thud of big hooves on hard ground, drag of brakes[4] and the jingle of trace chains. Men were calling back and forth from the teams. George, sitting on the bunk beside Lennie, frowned[5] as he thought. Lennie asked timidly, "You ain't mad[6], George?"

"I ain't mad at you. I'm mad at this here Curley bastard. I hoped we was gonna get a little stake together[7]—maybe a hundred dollars." His tone grew decisive. "You keep away from Curley, Lennie."

"Sure I will, George. I won't say a word."

"Don't let him pull you in[8]—but—if the son-of-a-bitch socks you—let 'im have it[9]."

"Let 'im have what, George?"

"Never mind, never mind. I'll tell you when. I hate that kind of a guy. Look, Lennie, if you get in any kind of trouble, you remember what I told you to do?"

Lennie raised up on his elbow. His face contorted[10] with thought. Then his eyes moved sadly to George's

1. **you move clear** tu dégages

2. **mourned** gémit

3. **to plug himself up** se faire mousser

4. **thud of big hooves on hard ground, drag of brakes** le bruit sourd de gros sabots sur le sol, le grincement des freins
5. **frowned** fronça les sourcils
6. **you ain't mad** t'es pas fâché

7. **get a little stake together** mettre un petit quelque chose de côté

8. **pull you in** te provoquer
9. **let 'im have it** rends-lui la pareille

10. **contorted** se contracta

face. "If I get in any trouble, you ain't gonna let me tend the rabbits."

"That's not what I meant. You remember where we slep'[1] last night? Down by the river?"

1. slep' = slept

"Yeah. I remember. Oh, sure I remember! I go there an' hide in the brush."

"Hide till I come for you. Don't let nobody see you. Hide in the brush by the river. Say that over[2]."

2. say that over répète

"Hide in the brush by the river, down in the brush by the river."

"If you get in trouble."

"If I get in trouble."

A brake screeched[3] outside. A call came, "Stable— Buck. Oh! Sta-able Buck."

3. a brake screeched un frein grinça

George said, "Say it over to yourself, Lennie, so you won't forget it."

Both men glanced up[4], for the rectangle of sunshine in the doorway was cut off. A girl was standing there looking in. She had full, rouged lips and wide-spaced eyes, heavily made up[5]. Her fingernails were red. Her hair hung in little rolled clusters[6], like sausages. She wore a cotton house dress and red mules, on the insteps[7] of which were little bouquets of red ostrich feathers[8]. "I'm lookin' for Curley," she said. Her voice had a nasal, brittle[9] quality.

4. glanced up levèrent les yeux

5. made up maquillés

6. rolled clusters grappes bouclées
7. insteps cous-de-pied

8. feathers plumes

9. brittle frêle

George looked away from her and then back. "He was in here a minute ago, but he went."

"Oh!" She put her hands behind her back and leaned against[10] the door frame so that her body was

10. leaned against s'appuya contre

1. **thrown forward** mis en avant

2. **bridled** se cambra

3. **playfully** d'un ton taquin

4. **archly and twitched** malicieusement et remua
5. **blame** reprocher

6. **goodlookin'** beauté

7. **apprehensive** inquiète

8. **tramp** traînée

9. **got his work ahead of him** va en voir de toutes les couleurs
10. **clear out** = leave for good

thrown forward[1]. "You're the new fellas that just come, ain't ya?"

"Yeah."

Lennie's eyes moved down over her body, and though she did not seem to be looking at Lennie she bridled[2] a little. She looked at her fingernails. "Sometimes Curley's in here," she explained.

George said brusquely, "Well he ain't now."

"If he ain't, I guess I better look someplace else," she said playfully[3].

Lennie watched her, fascinated. George said, "If I see him, I'll pass the word you was looking for him."

She smiled archly and twitched[4] her body. "Nobody can't blame[5] a person for lookin'," she said. There were footsteps behind her, going by. She turned her head. "Hi, Slim," she said.

Slim's voice came through the door. "Hi, Goodlookin'[6]."

"I'm tryin' to find Curley, Slim."

"Well, you ain't tryin' very hard. I seen him goin' in your house."

She was suddenly apprehensive[7]. "'Bye, boys," she called into the bunk house, and she hurried away.

George looked around at Lennie. "Jesus, what a tramp[8]," he said. "So that's what Curley picks for a wife."

"She's purty," said Lennie defensively.

"Yeah, and she's sure hidin' it. Curley got his work ahead of him[9]. Bet she'd clear out[10] for twenty bucks."

Lennie still stared at the doorway where she had been. "Gosh, she was purty." He smiled admiringly. George looked quickly down at him and then he took him by an ear and shook him.

"Listen to me, you crazy bastard," he said fiercely[1]. "Don't you even take a look at that bitch. I don't care what she says and what she does. I seen 'em poison before, but I never seen no piece of jail bait[2] worse than her. You leave her be."

Lennie tried to disengage his ear. "I never done nothing, George."

"No, you never. But when she was standin' in the doorway showin' her legs, you wasn't lookin' the other way, neither."

"I never meant no harm, George. Honest I never."

"Well, you keep away from her, 'cause she's a rattrap[3] if I ever seen one. You let Curley take the rap[4]. He let himself in for it. Glove fulla Vaseline," George said disgustedly. "An' I bet he's eatin' raw[5] eggs and writin' to the patent medicine houses[6]."

Lennie cried out suddenly—"I don' like this place, George. This ain't no good place. I wanna get outta here."

"We gotta keep it till we get a stake. We can't help it, Lennie. We'll get out jus' as soon as we can. I don't like it no better than you do." He went back to the table and set out a new solitaire hand. "No, I don't like it," he said. "For two bits I'd shove out of here[7]. If we can get jus' a few dollars in the poke[8] we'll shove off[9] and

1. **fiercely** avec force

2. **no piece of jail bait** un ticket pour la taule

3. **rattrap** piège à rats
4. **take the rap** se faire coincer

5. **raw** cru

6. **to the patent medicine houses** à toutes les pharmacies

7. **for two bits I'd shove out of here** je me barrerais pour trois fois rien
8. **in the poke** dans la poche
9. **shove off** = leave

43

go up the American River and pan gold[1]. We can make maybe a couple of dollars a day there, and we might hit a pocket[2]."

Lennie leaned eagerly[3] toward him. "Le's go, George. Le's get outta here. It's mean[4] here."

"We gotta stay," George said shortly[5]. "Shut up now. The guys'll be comin' in."

From the washroom nearby came the sound of running water and rattling[6] basins. George studied the cards. "Maybe we oughtta wash up," he said. "But we ain't done nothing to get dirty."

A tall man stood in the doorway. He held a crushed[7] Stetson hat under his arm while he combed[8] his long, black, damp[9] hair straight back. Like the others he wore blue jeans and a short denim jacket. When he had finished combing his hair he moved into the room, and he moved with a majesty only achieved[10] by royalty and master craftsmen[11]. He was a jerkline skinner, the prince of the ranch, capable of driving ten, sixteen, even twenty mules with a single line to the leaders. He was capable of killing a fly on the wheeler's butt[12] with a bull whip without touching the mule. There was a gravity in his manner and a quiet[13] so profound that all talk stopped when he spoke. His authority was so great that his word was taken on any subject, be it[14] politics or love. This was Slim, the jerkline skinner. His hatchet face[15] was ageless. He might have been thirty-five or fifty. His ear heard more than was said to him, and his slow speech had overtones[1] not of thought, but of under-standing beyond thought. His hands, large and lean[2], were as delicate in their action as those of a temple dancer.

He smoothed out his crushed hat, creased it[3] in the middle and put it on. He looked kindly[4] at the two in the bunk house. "It's brighter'n a bitch[5] outside," he said gently. "Can't hardly see nothing in here. You the new guys?"

"Just come," said George.

"Gonna buck barley?" "That's what the boss says."

Slim sat down on a box across the table from George. He studied the solitaire hand that was upside down to him. "Hope you get on my team," he said. His voice was very gentle[6]. "I gotta pair of punks on my team that don't know a barley bag from a blue ball[7]. You guys ever bucked any barley?"

"Hell, yes," said George. "I ain't nothing to scream about, but that big bastard there can put up more grain alone than most pairs can."

Lennie, who had been following the conversation back and forth with his eyes, smiled complacently[8] at the compliment. Slim looked approvingly[9] at George for having given the compliment. He leaned[10] over the table and snapped the corner of a loose card. "You guys travel around together?" His tone was friendly. It invited confidence without demanding it.

"Sure," said George. "We kinda look after each other." He indicated Lennie with his thumb. "He ain't

---

1. had overtones résonnait
2. lean fines
3. creased it marqua le pli
4. kindly avec bienveillance
5. brighter'n a bitch = very sunny
6. gentle douce
7. don't know a barley bag from a blue ball ne savent pas reconnaître un sac d'orge
8. complacently avec complaisance
9. approvingly d'un air approbateur
10. leaned se pencha

1. **knew** = known

2. **through** à travers

3. **mused** dit d'un air songeur

4. **big-stomached** pansu

5. **from the scrubbing and dousing** après l'avoir frottée et lavée

6. **chuckled softly** eut un petit rire

7. **bitch** chienne

8. **slang her pups** a mis bas à ses chiots
9. **drowned** noyé

bright. Hell of a good worker, though. Hell of a nice fella, but he ain't bright. I've knew[1] him for a long time."

Slim looked through[2] George and beyond him. "Ain't many guys travel around together," he mused[3]. "I don't know why. Maybe ever'body in the whole damn world is scared of each other."

"It's a lot nicer to go around with a guy you know," said George.

A powerful, big-stomached[4] man came into the bunk house. His head still dripped water from the scrubbing and dousing[5]. "Hi, Slim," he said, and then stopped and stared at George and Lennie.

"These guys jus' come," said Slim by way of introduction.

"Glad ta meet ya," the big man said. "My name's Carlson."

"I'm George Milton. This here's Lennie Small."

"Glad ta meet ya," Carlson said again. "He ain't very small." He chuckled softly[6] at his joke. "Ain't small at all," he repeated. "Meant to ask you, Slim—how's your bitch[7]? I seen she wasn't under your wagon this morning."

"She slang her pups[8] last night," said Slim. "Nine of 'em. I drowned[9] four of 'em right off. She couldn't feed that many."

"Got five left, huh?"

"Yeah, five. I kept the biggest."

"What kinda dogs you think they're gonna be?"

"I dunno[1]," said Slim. "Some kinda shepherds[2], I guess. That's the most kind I seen around here when she was in heat[3]."

Carlson went on, "Got five pups, huh? Gonna keep all of 'em?"

"I dunno. Have to keep 'em a while so they can drink Lulu's milk."

Carlson said thoughtfully, "Well, looka here[4], Slim. I been thinkin'. That dog of Candy's is so God damn old he can't hardly walk. Stinks[5] like hell, too. Ever' time he comes into the bunk house I can smell him for two, three days. Why'n't you get Candy to shoot his old dog and give him one of the pups to raise up? I can smell that dog a mile away. Got no teeth, damn near blind[6], can't eat. Candy feeds him milk. He can't chew nothing else."

George had been staring intently[7] at Slim. Suddenly a triangle began to ring outside, slowly at first, and then faster and faster until the beat of it disappeared into one ringing sound. It stopped as suddenly as it had started.

"There she goes," said Carlson.

Outside, there was a burst[8] of voices as a group of men went by.

Slim stood up slowly and with dignity. "You guys better come on while they's still something to eat. Won't be nothing left in a couple of minutes."

Carlson stepped back to let Slim precede him, and then the two of them went out the door.

1. **dunno** = don't know
2. **shepherds** chiens de berger
3. **in heat** en chaleur
4. **looka here** = listen
5. **stinks** il pue
6. **blind** aveugle
7. **intently** attentivement
8. **burst** éclat

Lennie was watching George excitedly. George rumpled[1] his cards into a messy pile. "Yeah!" George said, "I heard him, Lennie. I'll ask him."

"A brown and white one," Lennie cried excitedly.

"Come on. Le's get dinner. I don't know whether he got a brown and white one."

Lennie didn't move from his bunk. "You ask him right away, George, so he won't kill no more of 'em."

"Sure. Come on now, get up on your feet."

Lennie rolled off his bunk and stood up, and the two of them started for the door. Just as they reached it, Curley bounced in[2].

"You seen a girl around here?" he demanded angrily.

George said coldly, "'Bout[3] half an hour ago maybe."

"Well what the hell was she doin'?"

George stood still[4], watching the angry little man. He said insultingly, "She said—she was lookin' for you."

Curley seemed really to see George for the first time. His eyes flashed[5] over George, took in his height, measured his reach[6], looked at his trim middle[7]. "Well, which way'd she go?" he demanded at last.

"I dunno," said George. "I didn't watch her go."

Curley scowled[8] at him, and turning, hurried out the door.

George said, "Ya know, Lennie, I'm scared I'm gonna tangle[9] with that bastard myself. I hate his guts[10]. Jesus Christ! Come on. They won't be a damn thing left to eat."

1. **rumpled** brouilla

2. **bounced in** entra en trombe

3. **'bout** = about

4. **still** immobile

5. **flashed** dardèrent

6. **measured his reach** le jaugea
7. **trim middle** taille ferme

8. **scowled** jeta un regard noir

9. **tangle** me fritter
10. **I hate his guts** il me revient pas

They went out the door. The sunshine lay in a thin line under the window. From a distance there could be heard a rattle of dishes.

After a moment the ancient dog walked lamely in through the open door. He gazed about with mild[1], half-blind eyes. He sniffed, and then lay down and put his head between his paws. Curley popped[2] into the doorway again and stood looking into the room. The dog raised his head, but when Curley jerked out[3], the grizzled head sank to the floor again.

1. **mild** doux

2. **popped** apparut

3. **jerked out** s'en alla brusquement

III

PREVIOUSLY ON...

résumé
des épisodes
précédents

Although there was evening brightness showing through the windows of the bunk house, inside it was dusk[1]. Through the open door came the thuds[2] and occasional clangs of a horseshoe game[3], and now and then the sound of voices raised in approval or derision.

Slim and George came into the darkening bunk house together. Slim reached up over the card table and turned on the tin-shaded electric light[4]. Instantly the table was brilliant with light, and the cone of the shade threw its brightness straight downward, leaving the corners of the bunk house still in dusk. Slim sat down on a box and George took his place opposite.

"It wasn't nothing," said Slim. "I would of had to drowned most of 'em anyways. No need to thank me about that."

George said, "It wasn't much to you, maybe, but it was a hell of a lot to him. Jesus Christ, I don't know how we're gonna get him to sleep in here. He'll want to sleep right out in the barn[5] with 'em. We'll have trouble keepin' him from getting right in the box with them pups."

"It wasn't nothing," Slim repeated. "Say, you sure was right about him. Maybe he ain't bright, but I never seen such a worker. He damn near killed his partner buckin' barley. There ain't nobody can keep up with him[6]. God awmighty I never seen such a strong guy."

George spoke proudly[7]. "Jus' tell Lennie what to do an' he'll do it if it don't take no figuring[8]. He can't think of nothing to do himself, but he sure can take orders."

1. **dusk** crépuscule
2. **thuds** bruits sourds
3. **horseshoe game** jeu de lancé de fer à cheval

4. **tin-shaded electric light** la lampe en fer-blanc

5. **barn** grange

6. **keep up with him** suivre son rythme
7. **proudly** fièrement

8. **figuring** réflexion

There was a clang of horseshoe on iron stake[1] outside and a little cheer of voices.

Slim moved back slightly so the light was not on his face. "Funny how you an' him string along together[2]." It was Slim's calm invitation to confidence.

"What's funny about it?" George demanded defensively.

"Oh, I dunno. Hardly[3] none of the guys ever travel together. I hardly never seen two guys travel together. You know how the hands[4] are, they just come in and get their bunk and work a month, and then they quit and go out alone. Never seem to give a damn about nobody. It jus' seems kinda funny a cuckoo[5] like him and a smart little guy like you travelin' together."

"He ain't no cuckoo," said George. "He's dumb as hell[6], but he ain't crazy. An' I ain't so bright neither, or I wouldn't be buckin' barley for my fifty and found[7]. If I was bright, if I was even a little bit smart, I'd have my own little place, an' I'd be bringin' in my own crops[8], 'stead of doin' all the work and not getting what comes up outta the ground." George fell silent. He wanted to talk. Slim neither encouraged nor discouraged him. He just sat back quiet and receptive.

"It ain't so funny, him an' me goin' aroun' together," George said at last. "Him and me was both born in Auburn. I knowed[9] his Aunt Clara. She took him when he was a baby and raised him up. When his Aunt Clara died, Lennie just come along with me out workin'. Got kinda used to each other after a little while."

1. **iron stake** piquet en fer

2. **string along together** trainez ensemble

3. **hardly** presque

4. **the hands** les journaliers

5. **cuckoo** barjot

6. **dumb as hell** con comme un manche à balais
7. **fifty and found** = $50 and food and lodging

8. **crops** récoltes

9. **knowed** = knew

53

"Umm," said Slim.

George looked over at Slim and saw the calm, Godlike eyes fastened[1] on him. "Funny," said George. "I used to have a hell of a lot of fun with 'im. Used to play jokes on 'im 'cause he was too dumb to take care of 'imself. But he was too dumb even to know he had a joke played on him. I had fun. Made me seem God damn smart alongside of him. Why[2] he'd do any damn thing I tol' him. If I tol' him to walk over a cliff[3], over he'd go. That wasn't so damn much fun after a while. He never got mad about it, neither. I've beat the hell outta him, and he coulda bust[4] every bone in my body jus' with his han's[5], but he never lifted a finger against me." George's voice was taking on the tone of confession. "Tell you what made me stop that. One day a bunch[6] of guys was standin' around up on the Sacramento River. I was feelin' pretty smart. I turns to Lennie and says, 'Jump in.' An' he jumps. Couldn't swim a stroke[7]. He damn near drowned before we could get him. An' he was so damn nice to me for pullin' him out. Clean forgot I told him to jump in. Well, I ain't done nothing like that no more."

"He's a nice fella," said Slim. "Guy don't need no sense to be a nice fella. Seems to me sometimes it jus' works the other way around. Take a real smart guy and he ain't hardly ever a nice fella."

George stacked the scattered cards[8] and began to lay out his solitaire hand. The shoes thudded[9] on the ground outside. At the windows the light of the evening still made the window squares bright.

1. **fastened** fixés

2. **why** à vrai dire

3. **cliff** falaise

4. **bust** péter

5. **han's** = hands

6. **a bunch** un tas

7. **a stroke** = at all

8. **stacked the scattered cards** empila les cartes éparses
9. **the shoes thudded** les fers tombaient avec un bruit sourd

"I ain't got no people[1]," George said. "I seen the guys that go around on the ranches alone. That ain't no good. They don't have no fun. After a long time they get mean. They get wantin' to fight all the time."

"Yeah, they get mean," Slim agreed. "They get so they don't want to talk to nobody."

"'Course Lennie's a God damn nuisance[2] most of the time," said George. "But you get used to goin' around with a guy an' you can't get rid of[3] him."

"He ain't mean," said Slim. "I can see Lennie ain't a bit mean[4]."

"'Course he ain't mean. But he gets in trouble alla[5] time because he's so God damn dumb. Like what happened in Weed——" He stopped, stopped in the middle of turning over a card. He looked alarmed and peered over at[6] Slim. "You wouldn't tell nobody?"

"What'd he do in Weed?" Slim asked calmly.

"You wouldn' tell? . . . No, 'course you wouldn'."

"What'd he do in Weed?" Slim asked again.

"Well, he seen this girl in a red dress. Dumb bastard like he is, he wants to touch ever'thing he likes. Just wants to feel it. So he reaches out to feel[7] this red dress an' the girl lets out a squawk[8], and that gets Lennie all mixed up[9], and he holds on 'cause that's the only thing he can think to do. Well, this girl squawks and squawks. I was jus' a little bit off[10], and I heard all the yellin'[11], so I comes running, an' by that time Lennie's so scared all he can think to do is jus' hold on. I socked him over the head with a fence picket[12] to make him let go. He was so

1. **people** = family

2. **nuisance** casse-pieds

3. **get rid of** te débarrasser de

4. **ain't a bit mean** = is not mean at all
5. **alla** = all the

6. **peered over at** scruta

7. **reaches out to feel** tend la main pour toucher
8. **squawk** braillement
9. **mixed up** confus

10. **a little bit off** un petit peu plus loin
11. **yellin'** cris

12. **fence picket** piquet d'une clôture

2. **level and unwinking**
   stables et ne
   sourcillaient pas

3. **rabbits in an' tells
   the law she been
   raped** fonce raconter à
   la police qu'elle a été
   violée
4. **start a party out**
   organisent une battue
5. **on'y** = only
6. **we scrammed outta
   there** on a foutu le
   camp

7. **grabbed me**
   m'attrapait

8. **I can tell** je peux sentir

9. **hunched way over**
   penché vers l'avant

10. **drew up** remonta .

scairt[1] he couldn't let go of that dress. And he's so God damn strong, you know."

Slim's eyes were level and unwinking[2]. He nodded very slowly. "So what happens?"

George carefully built his line of solitaire cards. "Well, that girl rabbits in an' tells the law she been raped[3]. The guys in Weed start a party out[4] to lynch Lennie. So we sit in a irrigation ditch under water all the rest of that day. Got on'y[5] our heads sticking out from the side of the ditch. An' that night we scrammed outta there[6]."

Slim sat in silence for a moment. "Didn't hurt the girl none, huh?" he asked finally.

"Hell, no. He just scared her. I'd be scared too if he grabbed me[7]. But he never hurt her. He jus' wanted to touch that red dress, like he wants to pet them pups all the time."

"He ain't mean," said Slim. "I can tell[8] a mean guy a mile off."

"'Course he ain't, and he'll do any damn thing I——"

Lennie came in through the door. He wore his blue denim coat over his shoulders like a cape, and he walked hunched way over[9].

"Hi, Lennie," said George. "How do you like the pup now?"

Lennie said breathlessly, "He's brown an' white jus' like I wanted." He went directly to his bunk and lay down and turned his face to the wall and drew up[10] his knees.

George put down his cards very deliberately. "Lennie," he said sharply[1].

1. **sharply** sévèrement

Lennie twisted his neck and looked over his shoulder. "Huh? What you want, George?"

"I tol' you you couldn't bring that pup in here."

"What pup, George? I ain't got no pup."

George went quickly to him, grabbed him by the shoulder and rolled him over. He reached down and picked the tiny puppy from where Lennie had been concealing it[2] against his stomach.

2. **had been concealing it** le cachait
3. **'um** = him

Lennie sat up quickly. "Give 'um[3] to me, George."

George said, "You get right up an' take this pup back to the nest[4]. He's gotta sleep with his mother. You want to kill him? Just born last night an' you take him out of the nest. You take him back or I'll tell Slim not to let you have him."

4. **to the nest** = near his mother

Lennie held out his hands pleadingly[5]. "Give 'um to me, George. I'll take 'um back. I didn't mean no harm, George. Honest I didn't. I jus' wanted to pet 'um a little."

5. **pleadingly** suppliant

George handed the pup to him. "Awright. You get him back there quick, and don' you take him out no more. You'll kill him, the first thing you know." Lennie fairly scuttled[6] out of the room.

6. **fairly scuttled** déguerpi fissa

Slim had not moved. His calm eyes followed Lennie out the door. "Jesus," he said. "He's jes' like a kid, ain't he."

"Sure he's jes' like a kid. There ain't no more harm in him than a kid neither, except he's so strong. I bet[7] he won't come in here to sleep tonight. He'd sleep right

7. **I bet** je parie

alongside that box in the barn. Well—let 'im. He ain't doin' no harm out there."

It was almost dark outside now. Old Candy, the swamper, came in and went to his bunk, and behind him struggled[1] his old dog. "Hello, Slim. Hello, George. Didn't neither of you play horseshoes?"

"I don't like to play ever' night," said Slim.

Candy went on, "Either you guys got a slug[2] of whisky? I gotta gut ache[3]."

"I ain't," said Slim. "I'd drink it myself if I had, an' I ain't got a gut ache neither."

"Gotta bad gut ache," said Candy. "Them God damn turnips[4] give it to me. I knowed they was going to before I ever eat 'em."

The thick-bodied[5] Carlson came in out of the darkening yard. He walked to the other end of the bunk house and turned on the second shaded light. "Darker'n hell in here," he said. "Jesus, how that nigger can pitch shoes[6]."

"He's plenty good," said Slim.

"Damn right he is," said Carlson. "He don't give nobody else a chance to win——" He stopped and sniffed the air, and still sniffing, looked down at the old dog. "God awmighty, that dog stinks. Get him outta here, Candy! I don't know nothing that stinks as bad as an old dog. You gotta get him out."

Candy rolled to the edge[7] of his bunk. He reached over and patted[8] the ancient dog, and he apologized, "I been around him so much I never notice how he stinks."

1. **struggled** se déplaçait avec difficulté
2. **a slug** une gorgée
3. **gut ache** mal au ventre
4. **turnips** navets
5. **thick-bodied** corpulent
6. **pitch shoes** lancer des fers à chevaux
7. **the edge** le bout
8. **patted** caressa

"Well, I can't stand him in here," said Carlson. "That stink hangs around even after he's gone." He walked over with his heavy-legged stride[1] and looked down at the dog. "Got no teeth," he said. "He's all stiff with rheumatism. He ain't no good to you, Candy. An' he ain't no good to himself. Why'n't you shoot him, Candy?"

The old man squirmed[2] uncomfortably. "Well—hell! I had him so long. Had him since he was a pup. I herded sheep[3] with him." He said proudly, "You wouldn't think it to look at him now, but he was the best damn sheep dog I ever seen."

George said, "I seen a guy in Weed that had an Airedale[4] could herd sheep. Learned it from the other dogs."

Carlson was not to be put off[5]. "Look, Candy. This ol' dog jus' suffers hisself[6] all the time. If you was to take him out and shoot him right in the back of the head—" he leaned over and pointed, "—right there, why he'd never know what hit him."

Candy looked about unhappily. "No," he said softly. "No, I couldn' do that. I had 'im too long."

"He don't have no fun," Carlson insisted. "And he stinks to beat hell[7]. Tell you what. I'll shoot him for you. Then it won't be you that does it."

Candy threw his legs off his bunk. He scratched the white stubble[8] whiskers on his cheek nervously. "I'm so used to him," he said softly. "I had him from a pup."

"Well, you ain't bein' kind to him keepin' him alive," said Carlson. "Look, Slim's bitch got a litter[9] right now.

---

1. **his heavy-legged stride** son pas lourd

2. **squirmed** remua

3. **I herded sheep** j'ai gardé les moutons

4. **Airedale** terrier

5. **was not to be put off** ne se laissa pas distraire
6. **hisself** = himself

7. **to beat hell** comme la mort

8. **stubble** barbe de trois jours

9. **a litter** une portée

I bet Slim would give you one of them pups to raise up, wouldn't you, Slim?"

The skinner had been studying the old dog with his calm eyes. "Yeah," he said. "You can have a pup if you want to." He seemed to shake himself free for speech[1]. "Carl's right, Candy. That dog ain't no good to himself. I wisht somebody'd shoot me if I got old an' a cripple[2]."

Candy looked helplessly at him, for Slim's opinions were law. "Maybe it'd hurt him," he suggested. "I don't mind takin' care of him."

Carlson said, "The way I'd shoot him, he wouldn't feel nothing. I'd put the gun right there." He pointed with his toe[3]. "Right back of the head. He wouldn't even quiver[4]."

Candy looked for help from face to face. It was quite dark outside by now. A young laboring man came in. His sloping shoulders[5] were bent forward and he walked heavily on his heels, as though he carried the invisible grain bag. He went to his bunk and put his hat on his shelf. Then he picked a pulp magazine[6] from his shelf and brought it to the light over the table. "Did I show you this, Slim?" he asked.

"Show me what?"

The young man turned to the back of the magazine, put it down on the table and pointed with his finger. "Right there, read that." Slim bent over[7] it. "Go on," said the young man. "Read it out loud."

" 'Dear Editor:' " Slim read slowly. " 'I read your mag for six years and I think it is the best on the market.

---

1. **shake himself free for speech** se secouer pour reprendre la parole

2. **a cripple** un infirme

3. **toe** bout de son pied

4. **quiver** frissonner

5. **sloping shoulders** épaules tombantes

6. **pulp magazine** journal à sensation

7. **bent over** se pencha

I like stories by Peter Rand. I think he is a whingding[1]. Give us more like the Dark Rider. I don't write many letters. Just thought I would tell you I think your mag is the best dime's worth I ever spent[2].' "

Slim looked up questioningly. "What you want me to read that for?"

Whit said, "Go on. Read the name at the bottom."

Slim read, " 'Yours for success, William Tenner.' " He glanced up at Whit again. "What you want me to read that for?"

Whit closed the magazine impressively[3]. "Don't you remember Bill Tenner? Worked here about three months ago?"

Slim thought... "Little guy?" he asked. "Drove a cultivator?"

"That's him," Whit cried. "That's the guy!"

"You think he's the guy wrote this letter?"

"I know it. Bill and me was in here one day. Bill had one of them books that just come. He was lookin' in it and he says, 'I wrote a letter. Wonder if they put it in the book!' But it wasn't there. Bill says, 'Maybe they're savin' it[4] for later.' An' that's just what they done. There it is."

"Guess you're right," said Slim. "Got it right in the book."

George held out his hand for the magazine. "Let's look at it?"

Whit found the place again, but he did not surrender his hold on it[5]. He pointed out the letter with his

1. a whingding = really great

2. the best dime's worth I ever spent ce qu'on s'achete de mieux avec 10 cents

3. impressively avec fierté

4. savin' it la gardent

5. did not surrender his hold on it ne lâcha pas prise

1. **forefinger** index

2. **patch of field peas** champ de pois

3. **to be drawn in** de se laisser distraire

4. **a Luger** = a semi-automatic pistol
5. **none at all** = at all

6. **tomorra** = tomorrow

7. **reversal** revirement

8. **ceiling** plafond

9. **thong** lanière

forefinger[1]. And then he went to his box shelf and laid the magazine carefully in. "I wonder if Bill seen it," he said. "Bill and me worked in that patch of field peas[2]. Run cultivators, both of us. Bill was a hell of a nice fella."

During the conversation Carlson had refused to be drawn in[3]. He continued to look down at the old dog. Candy watched him uneasily. At last Carlson said, "If you want me to, I'll put the old devil out of his misery right now and get it over with. Ain't nothing left for him. Can't eat, can't see, can't even walk without hurtin'."

Candy said hopefully, "You ain't got no gun."

"The hell I ain't. Got a Luger[4]. It won't hurt him none at all[5]."

Candy said, "Maybe tomorra[6]. Le's wait till tomorra."

"I don't see no reason for it," said Carlson. He went to his bunk, pulled his bag from underneath it and took out a Luger pistol. "Let's get it over with," he said. "We can't sleep with him stinkin' around in here." He put the pistol in his hip pocket.

Candy looked a long time at Slim to try to find some reversal[7]. And Slim gave him none. At last Candy said softly and hopelessly, "Awright—take 'im." He did not look down at the dog at all. He lay back on his bunk and crossed his arms behind his head and stared at the ceiling[8].

From his pocket Carlson took a little leather thong[9]. He stooped over and tied it around the old dog's neck. All the men except Candy watched him. "Come boy.

Come on, boy," he said gently. And he said apologetically to Candy, "He won't even feel it." Candy did not move nor answer him. He twitched[1] the thong. "Come on, boy." The old dog got slowly and stiffly[2] to his feet and followed the gently pulling leash.

Slim said, "Carlson."

"Yeah?"

"You know what to do."

"What ya mean, Slim?"

"Take a shovel[3]," said Slim shortly.

"Oh, sure! I get you." He led the dog out into the darkness.

George followed to the door and shut the door and set the latch gently in its place. Candy lay rigidly on his bed staring at the ceiling.

Slim said loudly, "One of my lead mules got a bad hoof[4]. Got to get some tar[5] on it." His voice trailed off[6]. It was silent outside. Carlson's footsteps died away. The silence came into the room. And the silence lasted[7].

George chuckled, "I bet Lennie's right out there in the barn with his pup. He won't want to come in here no more now he's got a pup."

Slim said, "Candy, you can have any one of them pups you want."

Candy did not answer. The silence fell on the room again. It came out of the night and invaded the room. George said, "Anybody like to play a little euchre[8]?"

"I'll play out a few with you," said Whit.

1. **twitched** remua
2. **stiffly** avec raideur
3. **shovel** pelle
4. **hoof** sabot
5. **tar** goudron
6. **trailed off** s'évanouit
7. **lasted** dura
8. **euchre** = a card game

1. **rippled the edge of the deck** tritura le côté du paquet

2. **subdued** couvrit

3. **gnawing sound** bruit de grignotement
4. **gratefully** avec soulagement

5. **tightly** bien serrées

6. **dealt them** les distribua

7. **a scoring board** un tableau des scores
8. **pegs** taquets en bois (pour marquer les points)

They took places opposite each other at the table under the light, but George did not shuffle the cards. He rippled the edge of the deck[1] nervously, and the little snapping noise drew the eyes of all the men in the room, so that he stopped doing it. The silence fell on the room again. A minute passed, and another minute. Candy lay still, staring at the ceiling. Slim gazed at him for a moment and then looked down at his hands; he subdued[2] one hand with the other, and held it down. There came a little gnawing sound[3] from under the floor and all the men looked down toward it gratefully[4]. Only Candy continued to stare at the ceiling.

"Sounds like there was a rat under there," said George. "We oughtta get a trap down there."

Whit broke out, "What the hell's takin' him so long? Lay out some cards, why don't you? We ain't going to get no euchre played this way."

George brought the cards together tightly[5] and studied the backs of them. The silence was in the room again.

A shot sounded in the distance. The men looked quickly at the old man. Every head turned toward him.

For a moment he continued to stare at the ceiling. Then he rolled slowly over and faced the wall and lay silent.

George shuffled the cards noisily and dealt them[6]. Whit drew a scoring board[7] to him and set the pegs[8] to start. Whit said, "I guess you guys really come here to work."

"How do ya mean?" George asked.

Whit laughed. "Well, ya come on a Friday. You got two days to work till Sunday."

"I don't see how you figure[1]," said George.

Whit laughed again. "You do if you been around these big ranches much. Guy that wants to look over a ranch comes in Sat'day[2] afternoon. He gets Sat'day night supper an' three meals on Sunday, and he can quit Monday mornin' after breakfast without turning his hand[3]. But you come to work Friday noon. You got to put in a day an' a half no matter how you figure."

George looked at him levelly[4]. "We're gonna stick aroun'[5] a while," he said. "Me an' Lennie's gonna roll up a stake[6]."

The door opened quietly and the stable buck put in his head; a lean[7] negro head, lined with pain[8], the eyes patient. "Mr. Slim."

Slim took his eyes from old Candy. "Huh? Oh! Hello, Crooks. What's'a matter?"

"You told me to warm up tar[9] for that mule's foot. I got it warm."

"Oh! Sure, Crooks. I'll come right out an' put it on."

"I can do it if you want, Mr. Slim."

"No. I'll come do it myself." He stood up.

Crooks said, "Mr. Slim."

"Yeah."

"That big new guy's messin' around[10] your pups out in the barn."

1. **how you figure** comment tu fais ton calcul

2. **Sat'day** = Saturday

3. **without turning his hand** sans lever le petit doigt

4. **levelly** bien en face

5. **stick aroun'** rester

6. **roll up a stake** = save up some money

7. **lean** mince
8. **lined with pain** marquée par la douleur

9. **tar** goudron

10. **messin' around** traficote

1. **handlin'** manipule

"Well, he ain't doin' no harm. I give him one of them pups."

"Just thought I'd tell ya," said Crooks. "He's takin' 'em outta the nest and handlin'[1] them. That won't do them no good."

"He won't hurt 'em," said Slim. "I'll come along with you now."

George looked up. "If that crazy bastard's foolin' around too much, jus' kick him out, Slim."

Slim followed the stable buck out of the room.

George dealt and Whit picked up his cards and examined them. "Seen the new kid yet?" he asked. "What kid?" George asked.

2. **why** eh ben

"Why[2], Curley's new wife."

"Yeah, I seen her."

3. **a looloo** une bombe

"Well, ain't she a looloo[3]?"

"I ain't seen that much of her," said George.

4. **concealin'** cache

Whit laid down his cards impressively. "Well, stick around an' keep your eyes open. You'll see plenty. She ain't concealin'[4] nothing. I never seen nobody like her. She got the eye goin' all the time on everybody. I bet she even gives the stable buck the eye. I don't know what the hell she wants."

5. **casually** l'air de rien

George asked casually[5], "Been any trouble since she got here?"

6. **scooped it in** la récupéra

It was obvious that Whit was not interested in his cards. He laid his hand down and George scooped it in[6]. George laid out his deliberate solitaire hand—seven cards, and six on top, and five on top of those.

Whit said, "I see what you mean. No, they ain't been nothing yet. Curley's got yella-jackets in his drawers[1], but that's all so far. Ever' time the guys is around she shows up. She's lookin' for Curley, or she thought she lef' somethin' layin' around and she's lookin' for it. Seems like she can't keep away from guys. An' Curley's pants is just crawlin' with ants, but they ain't nothing come of it yet."

George said, "She's gonna make a mess[2]. They's gonna be[3] a bad mess about her. She's a jail bait all set on the trigger[4]. That Curley got his work cut out[5] for him. Ranch with a bunch of guys on it ain't no place for a girl, 'specially like her."

Whit said, "If you got idears[6], you oughtta come in town with us guys tomorra night."

"Why? What's doin'[7]?"

"Jus' the usual thing. We go in to old Susy's place. Hell of a nice place. Old Susy's a laugh—always crackin' jokes[8]. Like she says when we come up on the front porch las' Sat'day night. Susy opens the door and then she yells over her shoulder, 'Get yor[9] coats on, girls, here comes the sheriff.' She never talks dirty, neither. Got five girls there."

"What's it set you back?[10]" George asked.

"Two an' a half[11]. You can get a shot for two bits[12]. Susy got nice chairs to set in, too. If a guy don't want a flop[13], why he can just set in the chairs and have a couple or three shots and pass the time of day and Susy don't give a damn. She ain't rushin' guys through[14] and kickin' 'em out if they don't want a flop."

1. **yella-jackets in his drawers** des frelons dans son slip (= il est nerveux)
2. **make a mess** foutre le bordel
3. **they's gonna be** = there is going to be
4. **all set on the trigger** = ready to cause trouble
5. **cut out** tout prêt
6. **idears** = ideas (= des envies)
7. **what's doin'** = what's going on
8. **crackin' jokes** à faire des blagues
9. **yor** = your
10. **what's it set you back?** = how much is it?
11. **Two an' a half** = 2,5 dollars
12. **two bits** = 25 cents
13. **a flop** une passe
14. **ain't rushin' guys through** bouscule pas les gars

1. **the joint** l'endroit

2. **rag rug** vieux tapis

3. **Kewpie doll** poupée populaires aux US après la Grande Dépression
4. **parlor house** bordel

5. **gettin' burned** brûler les plumes

6. **bow-legged** les jambes arquées

7. **a crack** le coup

8. **goo-goos** = silly young men

9. **crept** se faufila

"Might go in and look the joint[1] over," said George.

"Sure. Come along. It's a hell of a lot of fun—her crackin' jokes all the time. Like she says one time, she says, 'I've knew people that if they got a rag rug[2] on the floor an' a Kewpie doll[3] lamp on the phonograph they think they're running a parlor house[4].' That's Clara's house she's talkin' about. An' Susy says, 'I know what you boys want,' she says. 'My girls is clean,' she says, 'an' there ain't no water in my whisky,' she says. 'If any you guys wanta look at a Kewpie doll lamp an' take your own chance gettin' burned[5], why you know where to go.' An' she says, 'There's guys around here walkin' bow-legged[6] 'cause they like to look at a Kewpie doll lamp.' "

George asked, "Clara runs the other house, huh?"

"Yeah," said Whit. "We don't never go there. Clara gets three bucks a crack[7] and thirty-five cents a shot, and she don't crack no jokes. But Susy's place is clean and she got nice chairs. Don't let no goo-goos[8] in, neither."

"Me an' Lennie's rollin' up a stake," said George.

"I might go in an' set and have a shot, but I ain't puttin' out no two and a half."

"Well, a guy got to have some fun sometime," said Whit.

The door opened and Lennie and Carlson came in together. Lennie crept[9] to his bunk and sat down, trying not to attract attention. Carlson reached under his bunk and brought out his bag. He didn't look at old Candy,

68

who still faced the wall. Carlson found a little cleaning rod[1] in the bag and a can of oil. He laid them on his bed and then brought out the pistol, took out the magazine and snapped the loaded shell[2] from the chamber. Then he fell to[3] cleaning the barrel with the little rod. When the ejector snapped, Candy turned over and looked for a moment at the gun before he turned back to the wall again.

Carlson said casually, "Curley been in yet?"

"No," said Whit. "What's eatin' on[4] Curley?"

Carlson squinted down[5] the barrel of his gun. "Lookin' for his old lady. I seen him going round and round outside."

Whit said sarcastically, "He spends half his time lookin' for her, and the rest of the time she's lookin' for him."

Curley burst[6] into the room excitedly. "Any you guys seen my wife?" he demanded.

"She ain't been here," said Whit.

Curley looked threateningly[7] about the room. "Where the hell's Slim?"

"Went out in the barn," said George. "He was gonna put some tar on a split hoof[8]."

Curley's shoulders dropped and squared[9]. "How long ago'd he go?"

"Five—ten minutes."

Curley jumped out the door and banged it[10] after him.

Whit stood up. "I guess maybe I'd like to see this," he said. "Curley's just spoilin'[11] or he wouldn't start for

---

1. **rod** petite baguette

2. **shell** cartouche

3. **he fell to** il se mit à

4. **what's eatin' on** = what's going on with
5. **squinted down** regardait d'un œil l'intérieur de

6. **burst** débarqua

7. **threateningly** d'un air menaçant

8. **split hoof** sabot fendu

9. **shoulders dropped and squared** baissa puis carra ses épaules

10. **banged it** la claqua

11. **just spoilin'** = just looking for a fight

Slim. An' Curley's handy, God damn handy. Got in the finals for the Golden Gloves. He got newspaper clippings[1] about it." He considered. "But jus' the same, he better leave Slim alone. Nobody don't know what Slim can do."

"Thinks Slim's with his wife, don't he?" said George.

"Looks like it," Whit said. "'Course Slim ain't. Least I don't think Slim is. But I like to see the fuss[2] if it comes off. Come on, le's go."

George said, "I'm stayin' right here. I don't want to get mixed up in nothing. Lennie and me got to make a stake."

Carlson finished the cleaning of the gun and put it in the bag and pushed the bag under his bunk. "I guess I'll go out and look her over," he said. Old Candy lay still, and Lennie, from his bunk, watched George cautiously.

When Whit and Carlson were gone and the door closed after them, George turned to Lennie. "What you got on your mind?"

"I ain't done nothing, George. Slim says I better not pet them pups so much for a while. Slim says it ain't good for them; so I come right in. I been good, George."

"I coulda told you that," said George.

"Well, I wasn't hurtin' 'em none. I jus' had mine in my lap pettin' it."

George asked, "Did you see Slim out in the barn?"

"Sure I did. He tol' me I better not pet that pup no more."

"Did you see that girl?"

"You mean Curley's girl?"

"Yeah. Did she come in the barn?"

"No. Anyways I never seen her."

"You never seen Slim talkin' to her?"

"Uh-uh. She ain't been in the barn."

"O.K.," said George. "I guess them guys ain't gonna see no fight. If there's any fightin', Lennie, you keep out of it[1]."

"I don't want no fights," said Lennie. He got up from his bunk and sat down at the table, across from George. Almost automatically George shuffled the cards and laid out his solitaire hand. He used a deliberate, thoughtful slowness[2].

Lennie reached for a face card and studied it, then turned it upside down and studied it. "Both ends the same," he said. "George, why is it both ends the same?"

"I don't know," said George. "That's jus' the way they make 'em. What was Slim doin' in the barn when you seen[3] him?"

"Slim?"

"Sure. You seen him in the barn, an' he tol' you not to pet the pups so much."

"Oh, yeah. He had a can a tar an' a paint brush. I don't know what for."

"You sure that girl didn't come in like she come in here today?"

"No. She never come."

George sighed[4]. "You give me a good whore house[5] every time," he said. "A guy can go in an' get drunk

1. **you keep out of it** tu t'en mêles pas

2. **thoughtful slowness** une lenteur réfléchie

3. **seen** = saw

4. **sighed** soupira
5. **whore house** bordel

1. **no messes** zéro problème

2. **just set on the trigger of the hoosegow** prêtes à vous envoyer direct en taule

3. **grammar school** l'école primaire
4. **hot cakes** crêpes

5. **his scoring rack** sa dernière rangée
6. **diamonds** carreaux
7. **San Quentin** = a prison

8. **drummed** pianota

9. **get a big stake together** mette un bon paquet de côté

10. **wide open** grands ouverts

and get ever'thing outta his system all at once, an' no messes[1]. And he knows how much it's gonna set him back. These here jail baits is just set on the trigger of the hoosegow[2]."

Lennie followed his words admiringly, and moved his lips a little to keep up. George continued, "You remember Andy Cushman, Lennie? Went to grammar school[3]?"

"The one that his old lady used to make hot cakes[4] for the kids?" Lennie asked.

"Yeah. That's the one. You can remember anything if there's anything to eat in it." George looked carefully at the solitaire hand. He put an ace up on his scoring rack[5] and piled a two, three and four of diamonds[6] on it. "Andy's in San Quentin[7] right now on account of a tart," said George.

Lennie drummed[8] on the table with his fingers. "George?"

"Huh?"

"George, how long's it gonna be till we get that little place an' live on the fatta the lan'—an' rabbits?"

"I don' know," said George. "We gotta get a big stake together[9]. I know a little place we can get cheap, but they ain't givin' it away."

Old Candy turned slowly over. His eyes were wide open[10]. He watched George carefully.

Lennie said, "Tell about that place, George."

"I jus' tol' you, jus' las' night."

"Go on—tell again, George."

"Well, it's ten acres[1]," said George. "Got a little win'mill. Got a little shack on it, an' a chicken run[2]. Got a kitchen, orchard, cherries, apples, peaches, 'cots[3], nuts, got a few berries. They's a place for alfalfa[4] and plenty water to flood it[5]. They's a pig pen[6]——"

"An' rabbits, George."

"No place for rabbits now, but I could easy build a few hutches[7] and you could feed alfalfa to the rabbits."

"Damn right, I could," said Lennie. "You God damn right I could."

George's hands stopped working with the cards. His voice was growing warmer. "An' we could have a few pigs. I could build a smoke house[8] like the one gran'pa had, an' when we kill a pig we can smoke the bacon and the hams, and make sausage an' all like that. An' when the salmon run up river we could catch a hundred of 'em an' salt 'em down or smoke 'em. We could have them for breakfast. They[9] ain't nothing so nice as smoked salmon. When the fruit come in we could can it[10]—and tomatoes, they're easy to can. Ever' Sunday we'd kill a chicken or a rabbit. Maybe we'd have a cow or a goat[11], and the cream is so God damn thick you got to cut it with a knife and take it out with a spoon."

Lennie watched him with wide eyes, and old Candy watched him too. Lennie said softly, "We could live offa the fatta the lan'."

"Sure," said George. "All kin's a[12] vegetables in the garden, and if we want a little whisky we can sell a few eggs or something, or some milk. We'd jus' live there.

1. **ten acres** = 4 000 m²
2. **win'mill** moulin à vent **little shack** petite maison **chicken run** poulailler
3. **'cots** = apricots
4. **alfalfa** de la luzerne
5. **flood it** l'arroser
6. **pen** enclos

7. **hutches** clapiers

8. **a smoke house** un fumoir

9. **they** = there

10. **can it** les mettre en conserve

11. **goat** chèvre

12. **kin's a** = kinds of

1. **we'd belong there** ça
serait notre chez-nous
2. **Jap** = Japanese

3. **begged** implora

4. **we put in a crop** on
planterait une récolte

5. **they'd nibble** ils
grignoteraient

6. **would throw a litter**
feraient des petits

7. **raptly** absorbé

8. **nobody could can us**
personne pourrait nous
virer

9. **fren'** = friend

We'd belong there[1]. There wouldn't be no more runnin' round the country and gettin' fed by a Jap[2] cook. No, sir, we'd have our own place where we belonged and not sleep in no bunk house."

"Tell about the house, George," Lennie begged[3].

"Sure, we'd have a little house an' a room to ourself. Little fat iron stove, an' in the winter we'd keep a fire goin' in it. It ain't enough land so we'd have to work too hard. Maybe six, seven hours a day. We wouldn't have to buck no barley eleven hours a day. An' when we put in a crop[4], why, we'd be there to take the crop up. We'd know what come of our planting."

"An' rabbits," Lennie said eagerly. "An' I'd take care of 'em. Tell how I'd do that, George."

"Sure, you'd go out in the alfalfa patch an' you'd have a sack. You'd fill up the sack and bring it in an' put it in the rabbit cages."

"They'd nibble[5] an' they'd nibble," said Lennie, "the way they do. I seen 'em."

"Ever' six weeks or so," George continued, "them does would throw a litter[6] so we'd have plenty rabbits to eat an' to sell. An' we'd keep a few pigeons to go flyin' around the win'mill like they done when I was a kid." He looked raptly[7] at the wall over Lennie's head. "An' it'd be our own, an' nobody could can us[8]. If we don't like a guy we can say, 'Get the hell out,' and by God he's got to do it. An' if a fren'[9] come along, why we'd have an extra bunk, an' we'd say, 'Why don't you spen' the night?' an' by God he would. We'd have a setter dog and a couple stripe[1] cats, but you gotta watch out them cats don't get the little rabbits."

Lennie breathed hard[2]. "You jus' let 'em try to get the rabbits. I'll break their God damn necks. I'll . . . I'll smash 'em with a stick." He subsided[3], grumbling to himself, threatening the future cats which might dare to disturb[4] the future rabbits.

George sat entranced[5] with his own picture.

When Candy spoke they both jumped as though they had been caught doing something reprehensible. Candy said, "You know where's a place like that?"

George was on guard immediately. "S'pose I do," he said. "What's that to you?"

"You don't need to tell me where it's at. Might be any place."

"Sure," said George. "That's right. You couldn't find it in a hundred years."

Candy went on excitedly, "How much they want for a place like that?"

George watched him suspiciously. "Well—I could get it for six hundred bucks. The ol'[6] people that owns it is flat bust[7] an' the ol' lady needs an operation. Say— what's it to you? You got nothing to do with us."

Candy said, "I ain't much good with on'y one hand. I lost my hand right here on this ranch. That's why they give me a job swampin'[8]. An' they give me two hunderd[9] an' fifty dollars 'cause I los' my hand. An' I got fifty more saved up right in the bank, right now. Tha's three hunderd, and I got fifty more comin' the end

1. **stripe** tigrés

2. **breathed hard** respirait fort

3. **subsided** se calma

4. **might dare to disturb** oseraient déranger
5. **entranced** fasciné

6. **ol'** = old

7. **flat bust** complètement fauchés

8. **swampin'** comme homme à tout faire
9. **hunderd** = hundred

4. **will** testament
5. **my share** ma part
6. **kick off** = die

a the[1] month. Tell you what——" He leaned forward eagerly. "S'pose I went in with you guys. Tha's three hunderd an' fifty bucks I'd put in. I ain't much good, but I could cook and tend[2] the chickens and hoe[3] the garden some. How'd that be?"

George half-closed his eyes. "I gotta think about that. We was always gonna do it by ourselves."

Candy interrupted him, "I'd make a will[4] an' leave my share[5] to you guys in case I kick off[6], 'cause I ain't got no relatives nor nothing. You guys got any money? Maybe we could do her[7] right now?"

George spat[8] on the floor disgustedly. "We got ten bucks between us." Then he said thoughtfully[9], "Look, if me an' Lennie work a month an' don't spen' nothing, we'll have a hunderd bucks. That'd be four fifty. I bet we could swing her[10] for that. Then you an' Lennie could go get her started an' I'd get a job an' make up the res', an' you could sell eggs an' stuff like that."

They fell into a silence. They looked at one another, amazed[11]. This thing they had never really believed in was coming true. George said reverently, "Jesus Christ! I bet we could swing her." His eyes were full of wonder[12]. "I bet we could swing her," he repeated softly.

Candy sat on the edge of his bunk. He scratched the stump[13] of his wrist nervously. "I got hurt four years ago," he said. "They'll can me purty[14] soon. Jus' as soon as I can't swamp out no bunk houses they'll put me on the county[15]. Maybe if I give you guys my money, you'll let me hoe in the garden even after I ain't no good at it. An' I'll wash dishes an' little chicken stuff like that. But I'll be on our own place, an' I'll be let[1] to work on our own place." He said miserably, "You seen what they done to my dog tonight? They says he wasn't no good to himself nor nobody else. When they can me here I wisht somebody'd[2] shoot me. But they won't do nothing like that. I won't have no place to go, an' I can't get no more jobs. I'll have thirty dollars more comin', time you guys is ready to quit."

George stood up. "We'll do her[3]," he said. "We'll fix up[4] that little old place an' we'll go live there." He sat down again. They all sat still, all bemused[5] by the beauty of the thing, each mind was popped into[6] the future when this lovely thing should come about.

George said wonderingly, "S'pose they was a carnival or a circus come to town, or a ball game[7], or any damn thing." Old Candy nodded in appreciation of the idea. "We'd just go to her," George said. "We wouldn't ask nobody if we could. Jus' say, 'We'll go to her,' an' we would. Jus' milk the cow and sling[8] some grain to the chickens an' go to her."

"An' put some grass[9] to the rabbits," Lennie broke in. "I wouldn't never forget to feed them. When we gon'ta[10] do it, George?"

"In one month. Right squack[11] in one month. Know what I'm gon'ta do? I'm gon'ta write to them old people that owns the place that we'll take it. An' Candy'll send a hunderd dollars to bind her[12]."

1. an' I'll be let = and I'll be able

2. wisht somebody'd = wish that somebody would

3. we'll do her on va l'avoir
4. we'll fix up on arrangera
5. bemused déconcertés

6. popped into tendu vers

7. ball game = baseball game

8. sling jeter

9. grass herbe

10. gon'ta = going to

11. right squack exactement

12. bind her sceller la vente

77

"Sure will," said Candy. "They got a good stove there?"

"Sure, got a nice stove, burns coal or wood."

"I'm gonna take my pup," said Lennie. "I bet by Christ he likes it there, by Jesus."

Voices were approaching from outside. George said quickly, "Don't tell nobody about it. Jus' us three an' nobody else. They li'ble[1] to can us so we can't make no stake. Jus' go on like we was gonna buck barley the rest of our lives, then all of a sudden some day we'll go get our pay an' scram outta[2] here."

Lennie and Candy nodded, and they were grinning with delight[3]. "Don't tell nobody," Lennie said to himself.

Candy said, "George."

"Huh?"

"I oughtta of shot that dog myself, George. I shouldn't oughtta of[4] let no stranger shoot my dog."

The door opened. Slim came in, followed by Curley and Carlson and Whit. Slim's hands were black with tar and he was scowling[5]. Curley hung close to his elbow.

Curley said, "Well, I didn't mean nothing, Slim. I just ast[6] you."

Slim said, "Well, you been askin' me too often. I'm gettin' God damn sick of it. If you can't look after your own God damn wife, what you expect me to do about it? You lay offa me.[7]"

"I'm jus' tryin' to tell you I didn't mean nothing," said Curley. "I jus' thought you might of saw[8] her."

---

1. **li'ble** = liable (susceptibles)

2. **scram outta** = get out of

3. **were grinning with delight** = souriaient jusqu'aux oreilles

4. **shouldn't oughtta of** = should not have

5. **was scowling** avait l'air renfrogné

6. **ast** = asked

7. **lay offa me** = lay off of me = leave me alone

8. **of saw** = have seen

"Why'n't[1] you tell her to stay the hell home where she belongs?" said Carlson. "You let her hang around[2] bunk houses and pretty soon you're gonna have som'pin[3] on your hands and you won't be able to do nothing about it."

Curley whirled[4] on Carlson. "You keep outta this les' you wanta[5] step outside."

Carlson laughed. "You God damn punk," he said. "You tried to throw a scare[6] into Slim, an' you couldn't make it stick[7]. Slim throwed a scare inta you. You're yella[8] as a frog belly. I don't care if you're the best welter[9] in the country. You come for me, an' I'll kick your God damn head off."

Candy joined the attack with joy. "Glove fulla Vaseline," he said disgustedly. Curley glared[10] at him. His eyes slipped on[11] past and lighted on Lennie; and Lennie was still smiling with delight at the memory of the ranch.

Curley stepped over to Lennie like a terrier. "What the hell you laughin' at?"

Lennie looked blankly[12] at him. "Huh?"

Then Curley's rage exploded. "Come on, ya big bastard. Get up on your feet. No big son-of-a-bitch is gonna laugh at me. I'll show ya who's yella."

Lennie looked helplessly at George, and then he got up and tried to retreat. Curley was balanced and poised[13]. He slashed[14] at Lennie with his left, and then smashed down his nose with a right. Lennie gave a cry of terror. Blood welled[15] from his nose. "George," he

1.	**why'n't** = why don't
2.	**hang around** traîner autour des
3.	**som'pin** = something = a problem
4.	**whirled** se retourna brusquement
5.	**les' you wanta** = unless you want to
6.	**throw a scare** foutre la trouille
7.	**you couldn't make it stick** t'as pas réussi
8.	**yella** = yellow = a coward (un lâche)
9.	**welter** = welterweight = a boxer who weighs between 63 and 67 kilos
10.	**glared** lança un regard furieux
11.	**slipped on** glissèrent
12.	**blankly** sans comprendre
13.	**balanced and poised** bien campé sur ses pieds
14.	**slashed** décocha un coup
15.	**welled** jaillit

1. **backed** recula

2. **slugging him** le cognant
3. **frightened** effrayé

4. **bleated** gémit

5. **wind** souffle

6. **was flopping** pendouillait

7. **leggo** = let go

8. **slapped him** le baffa

9. **shrunken** affaissé

cried. "Make 'um let me alone, George." He backed[1] until he was against the wall, and Curley followed, slugging him[2] in the face. Lennie's hands remained at his sides; he was too frightened[3] to defend himself.

George was on his feet yelling, "Get him, Lennie. Don't let him do it."

Lennie covered his face with huge paws and bleated[4] with terror. He cried, "Make 'um stop, George." Then Curley attacked his stomach and cut off his wind[5].

Slim jumped up. "The dirty little rat," he cried, "I'll get 'um myself."

George put out his hand and grabbed Slim. "Wait a minute," he shouted. He cupped his hands around his mouth and yelled, "Get 'im, Lennie!"

Lennie took his hands away from his face and looked about for George, and Curley slashed at his eyes. The big face was covered with blood. George yelled again, "I said get him."

Curley's fist was swinging when Lennie reached for it. The next minute Curley was flopping[6] like a fish on a line, and his closed fist was lost in Lennie's big hand. George ran down the room. "Leggo[7] of him, Lennie. Let go."

But Lennie watched in terror the flopping little man whom he held. Blood ran down Lennie's face, one of his eyes was cut and closed. George slapped him[8] in the face again and again, and still Lennie held on to the closed fist. Curley was white and shrunken[9] by now, and his struggling had become weak[1]. He stood crying, his fist lost in Lennie's paw.

George shouted over and over, "Leggo his hand, Lennie. Leggo. Slim, come help me while the guy got any hand left."

Suddenly Lennie let go his hold. He crouched cowering[2] against the wall. "You tol' me to, George," he said miserably.

Curley sat down on the floor, looking in wonder[3] at his crushed hand. Slim and Carlson bent over him. Then Slim straightened up[4] and regarded Lennie with horror. "We got to get him in to a doctor," he said. "Looks to me like ever' bone in his han' is bust[5]."

"I didn't wanta," Lennie cried. "I didn't wanta hurt him."

Slim said, "Carlson, you get the candy wagon hitched up[6]. We'll take 'um into Soledad an' get 'um fixed up[7]." Carlson hurried out. Slim turned to the whimpering[8] Lennie. "It ain't your fault," he said. "This punk sure had it comin' to him. But—Jesus! He ain't hardly got no han' left." Slim hurried out, and in a moment returned with a tin cup[9] of water. He held it to Curley's lips.

George said, "Slim, will we get canned now? We need the stake. Will Curley's old man can us now?"

Slim smiled wryly[10]. He knelt down beside Curley. "You got your senses in hand enough to listen?" he asked. Curley nodded. "Well, then listen," Slim went on. "I think you got your han' caught in

1. **his struggling had become weak** il se débattait mollement maintenant

2. **cowering** recroquevillé

3. **in wonder** = with stupefaction

4. **straightened up** se redressa

5. **bust** pétés

6. **get the candy wagon hitched up** attelles la charrette
7. **fixed up** l'arranger
8. **whimpering** pleurnichant

9. **tin cup** tasse en fer blanc

10. **smiled wryly** grimaça

a machine. If you don't tell nobody what happened, we ain't going to. But you jus' tell an' try to get this guy canned and we'll tell ever'body, an' then will you get the laugh[1]."

"I won't tell," said Curley. He avoided looking at Lennie.

Buggy wheels[2] sounded outside. Slim helped Curley up. "Come on now. Carlson's gonna take you to a doctor." He helped Curley out the door. The sound of wheels drew away. In a moment Slim came back into the bunk house. He looked at Lennie, still crouched[3] fearfully against the wall. "Le's see your hands," he asked.

Lennie stuck out[4] his hands.

"Christ awmighty, I hate to have you mad at me," Slim said.

George broke in, "Lennie was jus' scairt[5]," he explained. "He didn't know what to do. I told you nobody ought never to fight him. No, I guess it was Candy I told."

Candy nodded solemnly. "That's jus' what you done," he said. "Right this morning when Curley first lit intil your fren'[6], you says, 'He better not fool with Lennie if he knows what's good for 'um.' That's jus' what you says to me."

George turned to Lennie. "It ain't your fault," he said. "You don't need to be scairt no more. You done jus' what I tol' you to. Maybe you better go in the washroom an' clean up your face. You look like hell."

Margin glossary:

1. **will you get the laugh** c'est de toi qu'on rira

2. **buggy wheels** les roues de la charrette

3. **crouched** accroupi

4. **stuck out** tendit

5. **scairt** = scared

6. **lit intil your fren'** = went after your friend

Lennie smiled with his bruised[1] mouth. "I didn't want no trouble," he said. He walked toward the door, but just before he came to it, he turned back. "George?"

"What you want?"

"I can still tend the rabbits, George?"

"Sure. You ain't done nothing wrong."

"I di'n't mean no harm, George."

"Well, get the hell out and wash your face."

1. **bruised** blessée

IV

PREVIOUSLY ON...

résumé
des épisodes
précédents

Crooks, the negro stable buck, had his bunk in the harness room; a little shed that leaned off[1] the wall of the barn. On one side of the little room there was a square four-paned[2] window, and on the other, a narrow plank door leading into the barn. Crooks' bunk was a long box filled with straw, on which his blankets were flung[3]. On the wall by the window there were pegs[4] on which hung broken harness in process of being mended[5]; strips of new leather; and under the window itself a little bench for leather-working tools[6], curved knives and needles and balls of linen thread, and a small hand riveter[7]. On pegs were also pieces of harness, a split collar with the horsehair stuffing sticking out, a broken hame[8], and a trace chain[9] with its leather covering split[10]. Crooks had his apple box over his bunk, and in it a range[11] of medicine bottles, both for himself and for the horses. There were cans of saddle[12] soap and a drippy[13] can of tar with its paint brush sticking over the edge. And scattered[14] about the floor were a number of personal possessions; for, being alone, Crooks could leave his things about, and being a stable buck and a cripple[15], he was more permanent than the other men, and he had accumulated more possessions than he could carry on his back.

Crooks possessed several pairs of shoes, a pair of rubber[16] boots, a big alarm clock and a single-barreled shotgun. And he had books, too; a tattered[17] dictionary and a mauled[18] copy of the California civil code for 1905. There were battered[19] magazines and a few dirty books on a special shelf over his bunk. A pair of large gold-rimmed spectacles[1] hung from a nail[2] on the wall above his bed.

This room was swept and fairly neat[3], for Crooks was a proud, aloof[4] man. He kept his distance and demanded that other people keep theirs. His body was bent over to the left by his crooked spine[5], and his eyes lay deep[6] in his head, and because of their depth seemed to glitter[7] with intensity. His lean[8] face was lined with deep black wrinkles[9], and he had thin, pain-tightened[10] lips which were lighter than his face.

It was Saturday night. Through the open door that led into the barn came the sound of moving horses, of feet stirring[11], of teeth champing on hay[12], of the rattle of halter chains[13]. In the stable buck's room a small electric globe threw a meager[14] yellow light.

Crooks sat on his bunk. His shirt was out of his jeans in back. In one hand he held a bottle of liniment[15], and with the other he rubbed[16] his spine. Now and then he poured[17] a few drops of the liniment into his pink-palmed hand and reached up under his shirt to rub again. He flexed his muscles against his back and shivered[18].

Noiselessly Lennie appeared in the open doorway and stood there looking in, his big shoulders nearly filling[19] the opening. For a moment Crooks did not see him, but on raising his eyes he stiffened[20] and a scowl[21] came on his face. His hand came out from under his shirt.

1. **gold-rimmed spectacles** lunettes à la monture dorée
2. **nail** clou
3. **swept and fairly neat** balayée et bien tenue
4. **proud, aloof** fier et réservé
5. **crooked spine** colonne vertébrale tordue
6. **deep** profondément
7. **glitter** briller
8. **lean** maigre
9. **wrinkles** rides
10. **pain-tightened** serrées par la douleur
11. **stirring** s'agitant
12. **champing on hay** mâchonnant du foin
13. **rattle of halter chains** cliquetis des licols
14. **meager** faible
15. **liniment** pommade
16. **rubbed** frottait
17. **poured** versait
18. **shivered** frissonnait
19. **filling** remplissant
20. **stiffened** se raidit
21. **a scowl** un air renfrogné

Lennie smiled helplessly in an attempt to make friends.

Crooks said sharply, "You got no right to come in my room. This here's my room. Nobody got any right in here but me."

1. **gulped** avala sa salive
2. **fawning** flatteur

Lennie gulped[1] and his smile grew more fawning[2]. "I ain't doing nothing," he said. "Just come to look at my puppy. And I seen your light," he explained.

"Well, I got a right to have a light. You go on get outta my room. I ain't wanted in the bunk house, and you ain't wanted in my room."

"Why ain't you wanted?" Lennie asked.

"'Cause I'm black. They play cards in there, but I can't play because I'm black. They say I stink. Well, I tell you, all of you stink to me."

3. **flapped** agita

Lennie flapped[3] his big hands helplessly. "Ever'body went into town," he said. "Slim an' George an' ever'body. George says I gotta stay here an' not get in no trouble. I seen your light."

"Well, what do you want?"

"Nothing—I seen your light. I thought I could jus'

4. **an' set** = and sit

come in an' set[4]."

5. **stared at** dévisagea

Crooks stared at[5] Lennie, and he reached behind him and took down the spectacles and adjusted them over his pink ears and stared again. "I don't know what you're doin' in the barn anyway," he complained. "You

6. **they's** = there is

ain't no skinner. They's[6] no call for a bucker to come into the barn at all. You ain't no skinner. You ain't got nothing to do with the horses."

"The pup," Lennie repeated. "I come to see my pup."

"Well, go see your pup, then. Don't come in a place where you're not wanted."

Lennie lost his smile. He advanced a step into the room, then remembered and backed to the door again. "I looked at 'em a little. Slim says I ain't to pet 'em very much."

Crooks said, "Well, you been takin' 'em out of the nest all the time. I wonder[1] the old lady don't move 'em someplace else."

"Oh, she don't care. She lets me." Lennie had moved into the room again.

Crooks scowled, but Lennie's disarming smile defeated him. "Come on in and set a while," Crooks said. "'Long as[2] you won't get out and leave me alone, you might as well set down." His tone was a little more friendly. "All the boys gone into town, huh?"

"All but old Candy. He just sets in the bunk house sharpening[3] his pencil and sharpening and figuring[4]."

Crooks adjusted his glasses. "Figuring? What's Candy figuring about?"

Lennie almost shouted, "'Bout the rabbits."

"You're nuts," said Crooks. "You're crazy as a wedge[5]. What rabbits you talkin' about?"

"The rabbits we're gonna get, and I get to tend 'em, cut grass an' give 'em water, an' like that."

"Jus' nuts," said Crooks. "I don't blame the guy you travel with for keepin' you outta sight[6]."

Lennie said quietly, "It ain't no lie. We're gonna do it. Gonna get a little place an' live on the fatta the lan'."

1. **I wonder** = I don't know why

2. **'long as** = as long as

3. **sharpening** à tailler
4. **figuring** faire des calculs

5. **crazy as a wedge** complètement dingo

6. **outta sight** hors de sa vue

89

1. **settled himself** s'installa
2. **nail keg** baril à clous
3. **hunched down** se plia

4. **ever' word's** = every word is
5. **chin** menton

6. **boring** scrutant

7. **for miles around** à des kilomètres à la ronde

Crooks settled himself[1] more comfortably on his bunk. "Set down," he invited. "Set down on the nail keg[2]."

Lennie hunched down[3] on the little barrel. "You think it's a lie," Lennie said. "But it ain't no lie. Ever' word's[4] the truth, an' you can ast George."

Crooks put his dark chin[5] into his pink palm. "You travel aroun' with George, don't ya?"

"Sure. Me an' him goes ever' place together."

Crooks continued. "Sometimes he talks, and you don't know what the hell he's talkin' about. Ain't that so?" He leaned forward, boring[6] Lennie with his deep eyes. "Ain't that so?"

"Yeah . . . sometimes."

"Jus' talks on, an' you don't know what the hell it's all about?"

"Yeah . . . sometimes. But . . . not always."

Crooks leaned forward over the edge of the bunk. "I ain't a southern negro," he said. "I was born right here in California. My old man had a chicken ranch, 'bout ten acres. The white kids come to play at our place, an' sometimes I went to play with them, and some of them was pretty nice. My ol' man didn't like that. I never knew till long later why he didn't like that. But I know now." He hesitated, and when he spoke again his voice was softer. "There wasn't another colored family for miles around[7]. And now there ain't a colored man on this ranch an' there's jus' one family in Soledad." He laughed. "If I say something, why it's just a nigger sayin' it."

Lennie asked, "How long you think it'll be before them pups will be old enough to pet?"

Crooks laughed again. "A guy can talk to you an' be sure you won't go blabbin'[1]. Couple of weeks an' them pups'll be all right. George knows what he's about[2]. Jus' talks, an' you don't understand nothing." He leaned forward excitedly. "This is just a nigger talkin', an' a busted-back[3] nigger. So it don't mean nothing, see? You couldn't remember it anyways. I seen it over an' over—a guy talkin' to another guy and it don't make no difference if he don't hear or understand. The thing is, they're talkin', or they're settin'[4] still not talkin'. It don't make no difference, no difference." His excitement had increased until he pounded[5] his knee with his hand. "George can tell you screwy[6] things, and it don't matter. It's just the talking. It's just bein' with another guy. That's all." He paused.

His voice grew soft and persuasive. "S'pose George don't come back no more. S'pose he took a powder[7] and just ain't coming back. What'll you do then?"

Lennie's attention came gradually to what had been said. "What?" he demanded.

"I said s'pose George went into town tonight and you never heard of him no more." Crooks pressed forward[8] some kind of private victory. "Just s'pose that," he repeated.

"He won't do it," Lennie cried. "George wouldn't do nothing like that. I been with George a long time. He'll come back tonight——" But the doubt was too much for him. "Don't you think he will?"

---

1. **blabbin'** répéter

2. **knows what he's about** sait de quoi il parle

3. **busted-back** au dos foutu

4. **settin'** = sitting

5. **pounded** martèle

6. **screwy** tordues

7. **took a powder** foute le camp

8. **pressed forward** cherchait à obtenir

1. **lighted** s'éclaira

Crooks' face lighted[1] with pleasure in his torture. "Nobody can't tell what a guy'll do," he observed calmly. "Le's say he wants to come back and can't. S'pose he gets killed or hurt so he can't come back."

Lennie struggled to understand. "George won't do nothing like that," he repeated. "George is careful. He won't get hurt. He ain't never been hurt, 'cause he's careful."

"Well s'pose, jus' s'pose he don't come back. What'll you do then?"

2. **wrinkled** se plissa

Lennie's face wrinkled[2] with apprehension. "I don' know. Say, what you doin' anyways?" he cried. "This ain't true. George ain't got hurt."

3. **bored in on him** = insisted
4. **booby hatch** = asylum

Crooks bored in on him[3]. "Want me ta tell ya what'll happen? They'll take ya to the booby hatch[4]. They'll tie ya up with a collar, like a dog."

5. **centered** s'immobilisèrent

Suddenly Lennie's eyes centered[5] and grew quiet, and mad. He stood up and walked dangerously toward Crooks. "Who hurt George?" he demanded.

Crooks saw the danger as it approached him. He edged back on his bunk to get out of the way. "I was just supposin'," he said. "George ain't hurt. He's all right. He'll be back all right."

6. **ain't nobody goin' to suppose** = nobody should be supposing
7. **wiped** essuya

Lennie stood over him. "What you supposin' for? Ain't nobody goin' to suppose[6] no hurt to George."

Crooks removed his glasses and wiped[7] his eyes with his fingers. "Jus' set down," he said. "George ain't hurt."

8. **growled** grogna

Lennie growled[8] back to his seat on the nail keg. "Ain't nobody goin' to talk no hurt to George," he grumbled.

Crooks said gently, "Maybe you can see now. You got George. You know he's goin' to come back. S'pose you didn't have nobody. S'pose you couldn't go into the bunk house and play rummy[1] 'cause you was black. How'd you like that? S'pose you had to sit out here an' read books. Sure you could play horseshoes till it got dark, but then you got to read books. Books ain't no good. A guy needs somebody—to be near him." He whined[2], "A guy goes nuts if he ain't got nobody. Don't make no difference who the guy is, long's he's with you. I tell ya," he cried, "I tell ya a guy gets too lonely an' he gets sick."

"George gonna come back," Lennie reassured himself in a frightened voice. "Maybe George come back already. Maybe I better go see."

Crooks said, "I didn't mean to scare you. He'll come back. I was talkin' about myself. A guy sets alone out here at night, maybe readin' books or thinkin' or stuff like that. Sometimes he gets thinkin', an' he got nothing to tell him what's so an' what ain't so[3]. Maybe if he sees somethin', he don't know whether it's right[4] or not. He can't turn to some other guy and ast him if he sees it too. He can't tell. He got nothing to measure by. I seen things out here. I wasn't drunk. I don't know if I was asleep. If some guy was with me, he could tell me I was asleep, an' then it would be all right. But I jus' don't know." Crooks was looking across the room now, looking toward the window.

Lennie said miserably, "George wun't[5] go away and leave me. I know George wun't do that."

1. **rummy** au rami (jeu de cartes)

2. **whined** geignit

3. **what's so an' what ain't so** = what is and what isn't
4. **right** = real

5. **wun't** = wouldn't

The stable buck went on dreamily, "I remember when I was a little kid on my old man's chicken ranch. Had two brothers. They was always near me, always there. Used to sleep right in the same room, right in the same bed—all three. Had a strawberry patch. Had an alfalfa patch. Used to turn the chickens out[1] in the alfalfa on a sunny morning. My brothers'd set on a fence rail[2] an' watch 'em—white chickens they was."

Gradually Lennie's interest came around to what was being said. "George says we're gonna have alfalfa for the rabbits."

"What rabbits?"

"We're gonna have rabbits an' a berry patch."

"You're nuts."

"We are too. You ast George."

"You're nuts." Crooks was scornful[3]. "I seen hunderds of men come by on the road an' on the ranches, with their bindles on their back an' that same damn thing in their heads. Hunderds of them. They come, an' they quit an' go on; an' every damn one of 'em's got a little piece of land in his head. An' never a God damn one of 'em ever gets it. Just like heaven. Ever'body wants a little piece of lan'. I read plenty of books out here. Nobody never gets to heaven, and nobody gets no land. It's just in their head. They're all the time talkin' about it, but it's jus' in their head." He paused and looked toward the open door, for the horses were moving restlessly[4] and the halter chains clinked. A horse whinnied[5]. "I guess somebody's out

1. **turn the chickens out** = let the chickens run
2. **fence rail** grillage
3. **scornful** plein de mépris
4. **restlessly** nerveusement
5. **whinnied** hennit

there," Crooks said. "Maybe Slim. Slim comes in sometimes two, three times a night. Slim's a real skinner. He looks out for his team." He pulled himself painfully upright[1] and moved toward the door. "That you, Slim?" he called.

Candy's voice answered. "Slim went in town. Say, you seen Lennie?"

"Ya mean the big guy?"

"Yeah. Seen him around any place?"

"He's in here," Crooks said shortly[2]. He went back to his bunk and lay down.

Candy stood in the doorway scratching his bald wrist[3] and looking blindly into the lighted room. He made no attempt to enter. "Tell ya what, Lennie. I been figuring out about them rabbits."

Crooks said irritably, "You can come in if you want."

Candy seemed embarrassed. "I do' know. 'Course, if ya want me to."

"Come on in. If everybody's comin' in, you might just as well." It was difficult for Crooks to conceal[4] his pleasure with anger.

Candy came in, but he was still embarrassed. "You got a nice cozy little place in here," he said to Crooks. "Must be nice to have a room all to yourself this way."

"Sure," said Crooks. "And a manure[5] pile under the window. Sure, it's swell[6]."

Lennie broke in, "You said about them rabbits."

Candy leaned against the wall beside the broken collar while he scratched the wrist stump[7]. "I been here

1. **painfully upright** péniblement debout

2. **shortly** sèchement

3. **bald wrist** moignon

4. **conceal** camoufler

5. **manure** fumier

6. **swell** = fantastic

7. **stump** moignon

a long time," he said. "An' Crooks been here a long time. This's the first time I ever been in his room."

Crooks said darkly[1], "Guys don't come into a colored man's room very much. Nobody been here but Slim. Slim an' the boss."

Candy quickly changed the subject. "Slim's as good a skinner as I ever seen[2]."

Lennie leaned toward the old swamper. "About them rabbits," he insisted.

Candy smiled. "I got it figured out. We can make some money on them rabbits if we go about it right[3]."

"But I get to tend 'em," Lennie broke in. "George says I get to tend 'em. He promised."

Crooks interrupted brutally. "You guys is just kiddin' yourself. You'll talk about it a hell of a lot, but you won't get no land. You'll be a swamper here till they take you out in a box[4]. Hell, I seen too many guys. Lennie here'll[5] quit an' be on the road in two, three weeks. Seems like ever' guy got land in his head."

Candy rubbed his cheek angrily. "You God damn right we're gonna do it. George says we are. We got the money right now."

"Yeah?" said Crooks. "An' where's George now? In town in a whore house. That's where your money's goin'. Jesus, I seen it happen too many times. I seen too many guys with land in their head. They never get none under their hand."

Candy cried, "Sure they all want it. Everybody wants a little bit of land, not much. Jus' somethin' that

---

was his. Somethin' he could live on and there couldn't nobody throw him off of it[1]. I never had none. I planted crops for damn near ever'body in this state, but they wasn't my crops, and when I harvested[2] 'em, it wasn't none of my harvest. But we gonna do it now, and don't make no mistake about that. George ain't got the money in town. That money's in the bank. Me an' Lennie an' George. We gonna have a room to ourself. We're gonna have a dog an' rabbits an' chickens. We're gonna have green corn an' maybe a cow or a goat." He stopped, overwhelmed[3] with his picture.

Crooks asked, "You say you got the money?"

"Damn right. We got most of it. Just a little bit more to get. Have it all in one month. George got the land all picked out[4], too."

Crooks reached around and explored his spine with his hand. "I never seen a guy really do it," he said. "I seen guys nearly crazy with loneliness for land, but ever' time a whore house or a blackjack game took what it takes." He hesitated. ". . . If you . . . guys would want a hand to work for nothing—just his keep[5], why I'd come an' lend a hand. I ain't so crippled I can't work like a son-of-a-bitch if I want to."

"Any you boys seen Curley?"

They swung[6] their heads toward the door. Looking in was Curley's wife. Her face was heavily made up[7]. Her lips were slightly parted[8]. She breathed strongly, as though she had been running.

"Curley ain't been here," Candy said sourly[9].

1. **throw him off of it** le jeter dehors

2. **harvested** récoltées

3. **overwhelmed** submergé

4. **all picked out** toute choisie

5. **just his keep** juste logé et blanchi

6. **swung** tournèrent d'un coup
7. **heavily made up** = with a lot of makeup
8. **slightly parted** légèrement entrouvertes

9. **sourly** d'un ton acerbe

She stood still in the doorway, smiling a little at them, rubbing the nails of one hand with the thumb and forefinger of the other. And her eyes traveled from one face to another. "They left all the weak ones here," she said finally. "Think I don't know where they all went? Even Curley. I know where they all went."

Lennie watched her, fascinated; but Candy and Crooks were scowling down away from her eyes[1]. Candy said, "Then if you know, why you want to ast us where Curley is at?"

She regarded them amusedly. "Funny thing," she said. "If I catch any one man, and he's alone, I get along fine[2] with him. But just let two of the guys get together an' you won't talk. Jus' nothing but mad." She dropped her fingers and put her hands on her hips[3]. "You're all scared of each other, that's what. Ever' one of you's[4] scared the rest is goin' to get something on you[5]."

After a pause Crooks said, "Maybe you better go along to your own house now. We don't want no trouble."

"Well, I ain't giving you no trouble. Think I don't like to talk to somebody ever' once in a while? Think I like to stick[6] in that house alla time?"

Candy laid the stump of his wrist on his knee and rubbed it gently with his hand. He said accusingly, "You gotta husban'. You got no call foolin' aroun' with other guys, causin' trouble."

The girl flared up[7]. "Sure I gotta husban'. You all seen him. Swell guy, ain't he? Spends all his time

1. **away from her eyes** évitant son regard

2. **fine** = well

3. **hips** hanches

4. **ever' one of you's** = all of you are
5. **is goin' to get something on you** ait quelque chose à raconter sur votre compte

6. **stick** rester coincée

7. **flared up** s'emporta

sayin' what he's gonna do to guys he don't like, and he don't like nobody. Think I'm gonna stay in that two-by-four house[1] and listen how Curley's gonna lead with his left twice, and then bring in the ol' right cross[2]? 'One-two' he says. 'Jus' the ol' one-two an' he'll go down.' " She paused and her face lost its sullenness[3] and grew interested. "Say—what happened to Curley's han'?"

There was an embarrassed silence. Candy stole a look[4] at Lennie. Then he coughed[5]. "Why . . . Curley . . . he got his han' caught in a machine, ma'am. Bust his han'."

She watched for a moment, and then she laughed. "Baloney[6]! What you think you're sellin' me[7]? Curley started som'pin'[8] he didn' finish. Caught in a machine—baloney! Why, he ain't give nobody the good ol' one-two since he got his han' bust. Who bust him?"

Candy repeated sullenly, "Got it caught in a machine."

"Awright," she said contemptuously[9]. "Awright, cover 'im up if ya wanta. Whatta[10] I care? You bindle bums[11] think you're so damn good. Whatta ya think I am, a kid? I tell ya I could of went with shows[12]. Not jus' one, neither. An' a guy tol' me he could put me in pitchers[13]. . ." She was breathless with indignation. "—Sat'day night. Ever'body out doin' som'pin'. Ever'body! An' what am I doin'? Standin' here talkin' to a bunch of bindle stiffs[14]—a nigger an' a dum-dum[15] and a lousy ol' sheep[16]—an' likin' it because they ain't nobody else."

1. **two-by-four house** = a tiny/cheap house

2. **right cross** coup du droit

3. **sullenness** air maussade

4. **stole a look** jeta un coup d'œil à la dérobée
5. **coughed** toussa

6. **baloney** foutaises
7. **sellin' me** = trying to make me believe
8. **som'pin'** = something

9. **contemptuously** avec dédain
10. **whatta** = what do

11. **bindle bums** clochards

12. **went with shows** = done théâtre

13. **pitchers** = the movies

14. **bindle stiffs** clodos
15. **dum-dum** abruti
16. **lousy ol' sheep** vieille brebis galeuse

Lennie watched her, his mouth half open. Crooks had retired into the terrible protective dignity of the negro. But a change came over old Candy. He stood up suddenly and knocked[1] his nail keg over backward. "I had enough," he said angrily. "You ain't wanted here. We told you you ain't. An' I tell ya, you got floozy idears[2] about what us guys amounts to. You ain't got sense enough in that chicken head to even see that we ain't stiffs. S'pose you get us canned. S'pose you do. You think we'll hit the highway[3] an' look for another lousy two-bit job[4] like this. You don't know that we got our own ranch to go to, an' our own house. We ain't got to stay here. We gotta house and chickens an' fruit trees an' a place a hunderd time prettier than this. An' we got fren's[5], that's what we got. Maybe there was a time when we was scared of gettin' canned, but we ain't no more. We got our own lan', and it's ours, an' we c'n[6] go to it."

Curley's wife laughed at him. "Baloney," she said. "I seen too many you guys. If you had two bits in the worl', why you'd be in gettin' two shots of corn[7] with it and suckin' the bottom of the glass[8]. I know you guys."

Candy's face had grown redder and redder, but before she was done speaking, he had control of himself. He was the master of the situation. "I might of knew[9]," he said gently. "Maybe you just better go along an' roll your hoop[10]. We ain't got nothing to say to you at all. We know what we got, and we don't care whether you know it or not. So maybe you better jus' scatter along[11]

---

1. **knocked** renversa

2. **floozy idears** = the wrong idea

3. **hit the highway** se remettrait sur la grand-route
4. **lousy two-bit job** un job pourri à deux balles

5. **fren's** = friends

6. **c'n** = can

7. **corn** = whiskey

8. **suckin' the bottom of the glass** lécheriez le fond de vos verres

9. **of knew** = have known

10. **roll your hoop** jouer au cerceau

11. **scatter along** déguerpir

now, 'cause Curley maybe ain't gonna like his wife out in the barn with us 'bindle stiffs.' "

She looked from one face to another, and they were all closed against her. And she looked longest at Lennie, until he dropped his eyes in embarrassment. Suddenly she said, "Where'd you get them bruises[1] on your face?"

Lennie looked up guiltily. "Who—me?"

"Yeah, you."

Lennie looked to Candy for help, and then he looked at his lap[2] again. "He got his han' caught in a machine," he said.

Curley's wife laughed. "O.K., Machine. I'll talk to you later. I like machines."

Candy broke in. "You let this guy alone. Don't you do no messing aroun' with him. I'm gonna tell George what you says. George won't have you messin' with Lennie."

"Who's George?" she asked. "The little guy you come with?"

Lennie smiled happily. "That's him," he said. "That's the guy, an' he's gonna let me tend the rabbits."

"Well, if that's all you want, I might get a couple rabbits myself."

Crooks stood up from his bunk and faced her. "I had enough," he said coldly. "You got no rights comin' in a colored man's room. You got no rights messing around in here at all. Now you jus' get out, an' get out quick. If you don't, I'm gonna ast the boss not to ever let you come in the barn no more."

1. **bruises** bleus

2. **lap** genoux

101

1. **in scorn** avec mépris

2. **trap** grande gueule

3. **strung up** pendu

4. **whip at him** s'en
prendre à lui
5. **averted** détournés

6. **drawn in** contenu

7. **framin'** tendant un
piège à

8. **subsided** céda

She turned on him in scorn[1]. "Listen, nigger," she said. "You know what I can do to you if you open your trap[2]?"

Crooks stared hopelessly at her, and then he sat down on his bunk and drew into himself.

She closed on him. "You know what I could do?"

Crooks seemed to grow smaller, and he pressed himself against the wall. "Yes, ma'am."

"Well, you keep your place then, nigger. I could get you strung up[3] on a tree so easy it ain't even funny."

Crooks had reduced himself to nothing. There was no personality, no ego—nothing to arouse either like or dislike. He said, "Yes, ma'am," and his voice was toneless.

For a moment she stood over him as though waiting for him to move so that she could whip at him[4] again; but Crooks sat perfectly still, his eyes averted[5], everything that might be hurt drawn in[6]. She turned at last to the other two.

Old Candy was watching her, fascinated. "If you was to do that, we'd tell," he said quietly. "We'd tell about you framin'[7] Crooks."

"Tell an' be damned," she cried. "Nobody'd listen to you an' you know it. Nobody'd listen to you."

Candy subsided[8]. "No . . ." he agreed. "Nobody'd listen to us."

Lennie whined, "I wisht George was here. I wisht George was here."

Candy stepped over to him. "Don't you worry none," he said. "I jus' heard the guys comin' in. George'll be in the bunk house right now, I bet." He turned to Curley's wife. "You better go home now," he said quietly. "If you go right now, we won't tell Curley you was here."

She appraised him coolly[1]. "I ain't sure you heard nothing."

"Better not take no chances[2]," he said. "If you ain't sure, you better take the safe way."

She turned to Lennie. "I'm glad you bust up Curley a little bit. He got it comin' to him[3]. Sometimes I'd like to bust him myself." She slipped out the door and disappeared into the dark barn. And while she went through the barn, the halter chains rattled, and some horses snorted[4] and some stamped[5] their feet.

Crooks seemed to come slowly out of the layers[6] of protection he had put on. "Was that the truth what you said about the guys come back?" he asked.

"Sure. I heard 'em."

"Well, I didn't hear nothing."

"The gate banged," Candy said, and he went on, "Jesus Christ, Curley's wife can move quiet[7]. I guess she had a lot of practice, though."

Crooks avoided[8] the whole subject now. "Maybe you guys better go," he said. "I ain't sure I want you in here no more. A colored man got to have some rights even if he don't like 'em."

Candy said, "That bitch didn't oughtta of said that to you."

1. **coolly** froidement

2. **take no chances** = risk it

3. **got it comin' to him** l'a bien cherché

4. **snorted** s'ébrouèrent
5. **stamped** tapèrent
6. **layers** couches

7. **quiet** discrètement

8. **avoided** esquivait

1. **dully** d'un ton amorphe

"It wasn't nothing," Crooks said dully[1]. "You guys comin' in an' settin' made me forget. What she says is true."

The horses snorted out in the barn and the chains rang and a voice called, "Lennie. Oh, Lennie. You in the barn?"

"It's George," Lennie cried. And he answered, "Here, George. I'm right in here."

In a second George stood framed in the door, and he looked disapprovingly about. "What you doin' in Crooks' room. You hadn't oughtta[2] be in here."

2. **hadn't oughtta** = shouldn't

Crooks nodded. "I tol' 'em, but they come in anyways."

"Well, why'n't you kick 'em out?"

"I di'n't care much," said Crooks. "Lennie's a nice fella."

3. **aroused himslef** s'excitait
4. **I got it doped out** = I figured out

Now Candy aroused himself[3]. "Oh, George! I been figurin' and figurin'. I got it doped out[4] how we can even make some money on them rabbits."

George scowled. "I though I tol' you not to tell nobody about that."

5. **crestfallen** dépité

Candy was crestfallen[5]. "Didn't tell nobody but Crooks."

George said, "Well you guys get outta here. Jesus, seems like I can't go away for a minute."

Candy and Lennie stood up and went toward the door. Crooks called, "Candy!"

"Huh?"

6. **'member** = remember
7. **hoein'** biner **doin' odd jobs** aider là où je peux

"'Member[6] what I said about hoein' and doin' odd jobs[7]?"

"Yeah," said Candy. "I remember."

"Well, jus' forget it," said Crooks. "I didn' mean it. Jus' foolin'[1]. I wouldn' want to go no place like that."

"Well, O.K., if you feel like that. Goodnight."

The three men went out of the door. As they went through the barn the horses snorted and the halter chains rattled.

Crooks sat on his bunk and looked at the door for a moment, and then he reached for the liniment bottle. He pulled out his shirt in back, poured a little liniment in his pink palm and, reaching around, he fell slowly to rubbing his back.

1. **jus' foolin'** je rigolais

V

PREVIOUSLY ON...

résumé
des épisodes
précédents

One end of the great barn was piled high with new hay and over the pile hung the four-taloned Jackson fork[1] suspended from its pulley. The hay came down like a mountain slope[2] to the other end of the barn, and there was a level place[3] as yet unfilled with the new crop. At the sides the feeding racks were visible, and between the slats[4] the heads of horses could be seen.

It was Sunday afternoon. The resting horses nibbled[5] the remaining wisps[6] of hay, and they stamped their feet and they bit the wood of the mangers[7] and rattled the halter chains. The afternoon sun sliced in through the cracks of the barn walls and lay in bright lines on the hay. There was the buzz of flies in the air, the lazy afternoon humming[8].

From outside came the clang of horseshoes on the playing peg and the shouts of men, playing, encouraging, jeering. But in the barn it was quiet and humming and lazy and warm.

Only Lennie was in the barn, and Lennie sat in the hay beside a packing case under a manger in the end of the barn that had not been filled with hay. Lennie sat in the hay and looked at a little dead puppy that lay in front of him. Lennie looked at it for a long time, and then he put out his huge hand and stroked it[9], stroked it clear from one end to the other.

And Lennie said softly to the puppy, "Why do you got to get killed? You ain't so little as mice. I didn't bounce you hard[10]." He bent the pup's head up and looked in its face, and he said to it, "Now maybe George

1. **the four-taloned Jackson fork** un grappin à quatre dents
2. **a mountain slope** le versant d'une montagne
3. **a level place** un espace libre
4. **slats** barreaux
5. **nibbled** mâchonnaient
6. **wisps** brindilles
7. **mangers** mangeoires
8. **humming** bourdonnement
9. **stroked it** le caressa
10. **bounce you hard** bousculé fort

ain't gonna let me tend no rabbits, if he fin's out you got killed."

He scooped a little hollow[1] and laid the puppy in it and covered it over with hay, out of sight[2]; but he continued to stare at the mound he had made. He said, "This ain't no bad thing like I got to go hide in the brush. Oh! no. This ain't. I'll tell George I foun' it dead."

He unburied the puppy and inspected it, and he stroked it from ears to tail. He went on sorrowfully[3], "But he'll know. George always knows. He'll say, 'You done it. Don't try to put nothing over on me.' An' he'll say, 'Now jus' for that you don't get to tend no rabbits!' "

Suddenly his anger arose. "God damn you," he cried. "Why do you got to get killed? You ain't so little as mice." He picked up the pup and hurled[4] it from him. He turned his back on it. He sat bent over his knees and he whispered, "Now I won't get to tend the rabbits. Now he won't let me." He rocked[5] himself back and forth in his sorrow[6].

From outside came the clang of horseshoes on the iron stake, and then a little chorus of cries[7]. Lennie got up and brought the puppy back and laid it on the hay and sat down. He stroked the pup again. "You wasn't big enough," he said. "They tol' me and tol' me you wasn't. I di'n't know you'd get killed so easy." He worked his fingers on the pup's limp[8] ear. "Maybe George won't care," he said. "This here God damn little son-of-a-bitch wasn't nothing to George."

1. **scooped a little hollow** fit un petit creux
2. **out of sight** hors de vue
3. **sorrowfully** tristement
4. **hurled** jeta violemment
5. **rocked** balança
6. **sorrow** chagrin
7. **chorus of cries** clameur
8. **limp** flasque

Curley's wife came around the end of the last stall[1]. She came very quietly, so that Lennie didn't see her. She wore her bright cotton dress and the mules with the red ostrich feathers. Her face was made up and the little sausage curls were all in place. She was quite near to him before Lennie looked up and saw her.

In a panic he shoveled[2] hay over the puppy with his fingers. He looked sullenly[3] up at her.

She said, "What you got there, sonny boy[4]?"

Lennie glared at her[5]. "George says I ain't to have nothing to do with you—talk to you or nothing."

She laughed. "George giving you orders about everything?"

Lennie looked down at the hay. "Says I can't tend no rabbits if I talk to you or anything."

She said quietly, "He's scared Curley'll get mad. Well, Curley got his arm in a sling[6]—an' if Curley gets tough[7], you can break his other han'. You didn't put nothing over on me about gettin' it caught in no machine."

But Lennie was not to be drawn[8]. "No, sir. I ain't gonna talk to you or nothing."

She knelt[9] in the hay beside him. "Listen," she said. "All the guys got a horseshoe tenement[10] goin' on. It's on'y about four o'clock. None of them guys is goin' to leave that tenement. Why can't I talk to you? I never get to talk to nobody. I get awful lonely."

Lennie said, "Well, I ain't supposed to talk to you or nothing."

"I get lonely," she said. "You can talk to people, but I can't talk to nobody but Curley. Else[1] he gets mad. How'd you like not to talk to anybody?"

Lennie said, "Well, I ain't supposed to. George's scared I'll get in trouble."

She changed the subject. "What you got covered up there?"

Then all of Lennie's woe[2] came back on him. "Jus' my pup," he said sadly. "Jus' my little pup." And he swept[3] the hay from on top of it.

"Why, he's dead," she cried.

"He was so little," said Lennie. "I was jus' playin' with him . . . an' he made[4] like he's gonna bite me . . . an' I made like I was gonna smack him[5] . . . an' . . . an' I done it. An' then he was dead."

She consoled him. "Don't you worry none. He was jus' a mutt[6]. You can get another one easy. The whole country is fulla mutts."

"It ain't that so much," Lennie explained miserably. "George ain't gonna let me tend no rabbits now."

"Why don't he?"

"Well, he said if I done any more bad things he ain't gonna let me tend the rabbits."

She moved closer to him and she spoke soothingly[7]. "Don't you worry about talkin' to me. Listen to the guys yell out there. They got four dollars bet[8] in that tenement. None of them ain't gonna leave till it's over."

"If George sees me talkin' to you he'll give me hell," Lennie said cautiously. "He tol' me so."

1. **else** ou bien

2. **woe** désespoir

3. **swept** balaya

4. **made** = looked

5. **smack him** lui donner une tape

6. **mutt** bâtard

7. **soothingly** sur un ton rassurant

8. **bet** de pariés

1. **wha's the matter** c'est
quoi le problème

2. **they ain't none of
them cares** tout le
monde s'en fout

3. **yet** encore
4. **tumbled out**
cascadèrent

5. **ol' lady** = mother

6. **coulda** = could have

7. **'nother** = another

8. **in pitchers** = in movies

9. **a natural** faite pour ça

Her face grew angry. "Wha's the matter[1] with me?" she cried. "Ain't I got a right to talk to nobody? Whatta they think I am, anyways? You're a nice guy. I don't know why I can't talk to you. I ain't doin' no harm to you."

"Well, George says you'll get us in a mess."

"Aw, nuts!" she said. "What kinda harm am I doin' to you? Seems like they ain't none of them cares[2] how I gotta live. I tell you I ain't used to livin' like this. I coulda made somethin' of myself." She said darkly, "Maybe I will yet[3]." And then her words tumbled out[4] in a passion of communication, as though she hurried before her listener could be taken away. "I lived right in Salinas," she said. "Come there when I was a kid. Well, a show come through, an' I met one of the actors. He says I could go with that show. But my ol' lady[5] wouldn' let me. She says because I was on'y fifteen. But the guy says I coulda[6]. If I'd went, I wouldn't be livin' like this, you bet."

Lennie stroked the pup back and forth. "We gonna have a little place—an' rabbits," he explained.

She went on with her story quickly, before she should be interrupted. "'Nother[7] time I met a guy, an' he was in pitchers[8]. Went out to the Riverside Dance Palace with him. He says he was gonna put me in the movies. Says I was a natural[9]. Soon's he got back to Hollywood he was gonna write to me about it." She looked closely at Lennie to see whether she was impressing him. "I never got that letter," she said. "I always thought my ol' lady stole it. Well, I wasn't gonna stay no place where

I couldn't get nowhere or make something of myself, an' where they stole your letters. I ast her if she stole it, too, an' she says no. So I married Curley. Met him out to the Riverside Dance Palace that same night." She demanded, "You listenin'?"

"Me? Sure."

"Well, I ain't told this to nobody before. Maybe I ought'n to[1]. I don' like Curley. He ain't a nice fella." And because she had confided[2] in him, she moved closer to Lennie and sat beside him. "Coulda been in the movies, an' had nice clothes—all them nice clothes like they wear. An' I coulda sat in them big hotels, an' had pitchers[3] took of me. When they had them previews I coulda went to them, an' spoke in the radio, an' it wouldn'ta cost me a cent because I was in the pitcher. An' all them nice clothes like they wear. Because this guy says I was a natural." She looked up at Lennie, and she made a small grand[4] gesture with her arm and hand to show that she could act. The fingers trailed after[5] her leading wrist, and her little finger stuck out grandly from the rest.

Lennie sighed deeply[6]. From outside came the clang of a horseshoe on metal, and then a chorus of cheers. "Somebody made a ringer[7]," said Curley's wife.

Now the light was lifting[8] as the sun went down, and the sun streaks climbed up[9] the wall and fell over the feeding racks and over the heads of the horses.

Lennie said, "Maybe if I took this pup out and throwed[10] him away George wouldn't never know. An' then I could tend the rabbits without no trouble."

1. **ought'n to** = shouldn't

2. **confided** confiée

3. **pitchers** = pictures

4. **grand** majestueux

5. **trailed after** = followed

6. **sighed deeply** soupira profondément

7. **made a ringer** a tapé dans le mille
8. **lifting** = moving up

9. **sun streaks climbed up** rayons de soleil grimpaient

10. **throwed** threw

Curley's wife said angrily, "Don't you think of nothing but rabbits?"

"We gonna have a little place," Lennie explained patiently. "We gonna have a house an' a garden and a place for alfalfa, an' that alfalfa is for the rabbits, an' I take a sack and get it all fulla alfalfa and then I take it to the rabbits."

She asked, "What makes you so nuts[1] about rabbits?"

Lennie had to think carefully before he could come to a conclusion. He moved cautiously close to her, until he was right[2] against her. "I like to pet nice things. Once at a fair I seen some of them long-hair rabbits. An' they was nice, you bet. Sometimes I've even pet mice, but not when I could get nothing better."

Curley's wife moved away from him a little. "I think you're nuts," she said.

"No I ain't," Lennie explained earnestly[3]. "George says I ain't. I like to pet nice things with my fingers, sof'[4] things."

She was a little bit reassured. "Well, who don't?" she said. "Ever'body likes that. I like to feel silk an' velvet[5]. Do you like to feel velvet?"

Lennie chuckled[6] with pleasure. "You bet, by God," he cried happily. "An' I had some, too. A lady give me some, an' that lady was—my own Aunt Clara. She give it right to me—'bout this big a piece. I wisht I had that velvet right now." A frown came over his face[7]. "I lost it," he said. "I ain't seen it for a long time."

1. **nuts** fana

2. **right** juste

3. **earnestly** avec sérieux

4. **sof'** = soft

5. **silk an' velvet** de la soie et du velours

6. **chuckled** pouffa

7. **a frown came over his face** il fronça les sourcils

Curley's wife laughed at him. "You're nuts," she said. "But you're a kinda nice fella. Jus' like a big baby. But a person can see kinda what you mean. When I'm doin' my hair sometimes I jus' set[1] an' stroke it 'cause it's so soft." To show how she did it, she ran[2] her fingers over the top of her head. "Some people got kinda coarse[3] hair," she said complacently[4]. "Take Curley. His hair is jus' like wire[5]. But mine is soft and fine[6]. 'Course I brush it a lot. That makes it fine. Here—feel right here." She took Lennie's hand and put it on her head. "Feel right aroun' there an' see how soft it is."

Lennie's big fingers fell to stroking her hair.

"Don't you muss[7] it up," she said.

Lennie said, "Oh! That's nice," and he stroked harder. "Oh, that's nice."

"Look out, now, you'll muss it." And then she cried angrily, "You stop it now, you'll mess it all up." She jerked her head sideways[8], and Lennie's fingers closed on her hair and hung on. "Let go," she cried. "You let go!"

Lennie was in a panic. His face was contorted[9]. She screamed then, and Lennie's other hand closed over her mouth and nose. "Please don't," he begged. "Oh! Please don't do that. George'll be mad."

She struggled[10] violently under his hands. Her feet battered on the hay and she writhed[11] to be free; and from under Lennie's hand came a muffled[12] screaming. Lennie began to cry with fright[13]. "Oh! Please don't do none of that," he begged. "George gonna say I done a

1. **set** = sit
2. **ran** passa
3. **coarse** rêches
4. **complacently** avec suffisance
5. **wire** du fil de fer
6. **fine** fins
7. **muss** = mess
8. **sideways** sur le côté
9. **contorted** contracté
10. **struggled** se débattit
11. **writhed** se tortilla
12. **muffled** étouffé
13. **with fright** d'effroi

1. **hoarse** rauque

2. **wild** fous

3. **flopped** remuait
4. **still** immobile

5. **nor** ni
6. **bent** se pencha

7. **bewildered** éberlué

8. **pawed up the hay**
entassa de la paille avec
ses grandes mains

9. **crouched down**
s'accroupit

10. **of did** = have done

11. **lay** gisait

bad thing. He ain't gonna let me tend no rabbits." He moved his hand a little and her hoarse[1] cry came out. Then Lennie grew angry. "Now don't," he said. "I don't want you to yell. You gonna get me in trouble jus' like George says you will. Now don't you do that." And she continued to struggle, and her eyes were wild[2] with terror. He shook her then, and he was angry with her. "Don't you go yellin'," he said, and he shook her; and her body flopped[3] like a fish. And then she was still[4], for Lennie had broken her neck.

He looked down at her, and carefully he removed his hand from over her mouth, and she lay still. "I don't want ta hurt you," he said, "but George'll be mad if you yell." When she didn't answer nor[5] move he bent[6] closely over her. He lifted her arm and let it drop. For a moment he seemed bewildered[7]. And then he whispered in fright, "I done a bad thing. I done another bad thing."

He pawed up the hay[8] until it partly covered her.

From outside the barn came a cry of men and the double clang of shoes on metal. For the first time Lennie became conscious of the outside. He crouched down[9] in the hay and listened. "I done a real bad thing," he said. "I shouldn't of did[10] that. George'll be mad. An' . . . he said . . . an' hide in the brush till he come. He's gonna be mad. In the brush till he come. Tha's what he said." Lennie went back and looked at the dead girl. The puppy lay[11] close to her. Lennie picked it up. "I'll throw him away," he said. "It's bad enough like it is." He put the pup under his coat, and he crept to the barn wall and peered out[1] between the cracks, toward the horse-shoe game. And then he crept around the end of the last manger and disappeared.

The sun streaks[2] were high on the wall by now, and the light was growing soft in the barn. Curley's wife lay on her back, and she was half covered with hay.

It was very quiet in the barn, and the quiet of the afternoon was on the ranch. Even the clang of the pitched shoes[3], even the voices of the men in the game seemed to grow more quiet. The air in the barn was dusky[4] in advance of the outside day. A pigeon flew in through the open hay door and circled and flew out again. Around the last stall came a shepherd bitch[5], lean and long, with heavy, hanging dugs[6]. Halfway to the packing box where the puppies were she caught[7] the dead scent of Curley's wife, and the hair rose[8] along her spine. She whimpered and cringed[9] to the packing box, and jumped in among the puppies.

Curley's wife lay with a half-covering of yellow hay. And the meanness and the plannings[10] and the discontent and the ache[11] for attention were all gone from her face. She was very pretty and simple, and her face was sweet and young. Now her rouged cheeks and her reddened lips made her seem alive and sleeping very lightly[12]. The curls, tiny little sausages, were spread on the hay behind her head, and her lips were parted[13].

As happens sometimes, a moment settled and hovered[14] and remained for much more than a moment.

1. **peered out** jeta un coup d'œil dehors
2. **sun streaks** rayons de soleil
3. **the pitched shoes** les fers lancés
4. **the air in the barn was dusky** la pénombre tombait dans la grange
5. **shepherd bitch** chienne de berger
6. **dugs** mamelles
7. **caught** sentit
8. **the hair rose** ses poils se hérissèrent
9. **whimpered and cringed** glapit et eut un mouvement de recul
10. **plannings** machinations
11. **the discontent and the ache** l'insatisfaction et le besoin
12. **sleeping very lightly** dormir d'un sommeil léger
13. **parted** entrouvertes
14. **settled and hovered** s'installa et flotta

And sound stopped and movement stopped for much, much more than a moment.

Then gradually time awakened again and moved sluggishly[1] on. The horses stamped[2] on the other side of the feeding racks and the halter chains clinked. Outside, the men's voices became louder and clearer.

From around the end of the last stall old Candy's voice came. "Lennie," he called. "Oh, Lennie! You in here? I been figuring some more. Tell you what we can do, Lennie." Old Candy appeared around the end of the last stall. "Oh, Lennie!" he called again; and then he stopped, and his body stiffened[3]. He rubbed his smooth wrist on his white stubble whiskers. "I di'n't know you was here," he said to Curley's wife.

When she didn't answer, he stepped nearer[4]. "You oughten[5] to sleep out here," he said disapprovingly; and then he was beside her and—"Oh, Jesus Christ!" He looked about helplessly, and he rubbed his beard. And then he jumped up and went quickly out of the barn.

But the barn was alive now. The horses stamped and snorted, and they chewed the straw of their bedding and they clashed the chains of their halters. In a moment Candy came back, and George was with him.

George said, "What was it you wanted to see me about?"

Candy pointed at Curley's wife. George stared[6]. "What's the matter with her?" he asked. He stepped closer, and then he echoed Candy's words. "Oh, Jesus Christ!" He was down on his knees beside her. He put

---

1. **sluggishly** lentement
2. **stamped** piétinèrent

3. **stiffened** se raidit

4. **stepped nearer** s'approcha
5. **oughten** = ought not

6. **stared** la fixa

his hand over her heart. And finally, when he stood up, slowly and stiffly, his face was as hard and tight[1] as wood, and his eyes were hard.

Candy said, "What done it?"

George looked coldly at him. "Ain't you got any idear[2]?" he asked. And Candy was silent. "I should of knew," George said hopelessly. "I guess maybe way back in my head[3] I did."

Candy asked, "What we gonna do now, George? What we gonna do now?"

George was a long time[4] in answering. "Guess . . . we gotta tell the . . . guys. I guess we gotta get 'im an' lock 'im up. We can't let 'im get away[5]. Why, the poor bastard'd starve[6]." And he tried to reassure himself. "Maybe they'll lock 'im up an' be nice to 'im."

But Candy said excitedly, "We oughtta let 'im get away. You don't know that Curley. Curley gon'ta wanta get 'im[7] lynched. Curley'll get 'im killed."

George watched Candy's lips. "Yeah," he said at last, "that's right, Curley will. An' the other guys will." And he looked back at Curley's wife.

Now Candy spoke his greatest fear. "You an' me can get that little place, can't we, George? You an' me can go there an' live nice, can't we, George? Can't we?"

Before George answered, Candy dropped his head and looked down at the hay. He knew.

George said softly, "—I think I knowed from the very first. I think I knowed we'd never do[8] her. He

1. **hard and tight** dur et contracté

2. **idear** = idea

3. **way back in my head** au fond de moi

4. **was a long time** = took a long time

5. **get away** s'échapper

6. **'d starve** mourrait de faim

7. **gon'ta wanta get 'im** = is going to want to get him

8. **do** = get

1. **usta** = used to
2. **got to** = started

3. **sulkily** sombrement

4. **lousy cat house** bordel pourri

5. **in meanness** par méchanceté

6. **straightened up** se redressa
7. **bring him in** l'arrêter

8. **in on it** = an accomplice

9. **his sorrow** sa peine

usta[1] like to hear about it so much I got to[2] thinking maybe we would."

"Then—it's all off?" Candy asked sulkily[3].

George didn't answer his question. George said, "I'll work my month an' I'll take my fifty bucks an' I'll stay all night in some lousy cat house[4]. Or I'll set in some pool-room till ever'body goes home. An' then I'll come back an' work another month an' I'll have fifty bucks more."

Candy said, "He's such a nice fella. I didn' think he'd do nothing like this."

George still stared at Curley's wife. "Lennie never done it in meanness[5]," he said. "All the time he done bad things, but he never done one of 'em mean." He straightened up[6] and looked back at Candy. "Now listen. We gotta tell the guys. They got to bring him in[7], I guess. They ain't no way out. Maybe they won't hurt 'im." He said sharply, "I ain't gonna let 'em hurt Lennie. Now you listen. The guys might think I was in on it[8]. I'm gonna go in the bunk house. Then in a minute you come out and tell the guys about her, and I'll come along and make like I never seen her. Will you do that? So the guys won't think I was in on it?"

Candy said, "Sure, George. Sure I'll do that."

"O.K. Give me a couple of minutes then, and you come runnin' out an' tell like you jus' found her. I'm going now." George turned and went quickly out of the barn.

Old Candy watched him go. He looked helplessly back at Curley's wife, and gradually his sorrow[9] and his anger grew into words. "You God damn tramp[1]," he said viciously[2]. "You done it, di'n't you? I s'pose you're glad. Ever'body knowed you'd mess things up. You wasn't no good. You ain't no good now, you lousy tart[3]." He sniveled[4], and his voice shook. "I could of hoed in the garden and washed dishes for them guys." He paused, and then went on in a singsong[5]. And he repeated the old words: "If they was a circus or a baseball game . . . we would of went to her . . . jus' said 'ta[6] hell with work,' an' went to her. Never ast nobody's say so[7]. An' they'd of[8] been a pig and chickens . . . an' in the winter . . . the little fat stove . . . an' the rain comin' . . . an' us jus' settin' there." His eyes blinded with tears and he turned and went weakly out of the barn, and he rubbed his bristly whiskers with his wrist stump.

Outside the noise of the game stopped. There was a rise of voices in question, a drum[9] of running feet and the men burst[10] into the barn. Slim and Carlson and young Whit and Curley, and Crooks keeping back out of attention range[11]. Candy came after them, and last of all came George. George had put on his blue denim coat and buttoned it, and his black hat was pulled down[12] low over his eyes. The men raced[13] around the last stall. Their eyes found Curley's wife in the gloom[14], they stopped and stood still and looked.

Then Slim went quietly over to her, and he felt her wrist[15]. One lean finger touched her cheek, and then his hand went under her slightly twisted[16] neck and his

1. **tramp** traînée
2. **viciously** avec rage

3. **you lousy tart** sale garce
4. **sniveled** renifla
5. **in a singsong** comme s'il psalmodiait

6. **ta** = to

7. **never ast nobody's say so** rien eu à demander à personne
8. **of** = have

9. **a drum** un martèlement
10. **burst** débarquèrent

11. **range** portée

12. **pulled down** rabattu

13. **raced** coururent

14. **the gloom** l'obscurité

15. **felt her wrist** prit son pouls
16. **slightly twisted** légèrement tordu

fingers explored her neck. When he stood up the men crowded near[1] and the spell was broken[2].

Curley came suddenly to life. "I know who done it," he cried. "That big son-of-a-bitch done it. I know he done it. Why—ever'body else was out there playin' horseshoes." He worked himself[3] into a fury. "I'm gonna get him. I'm going for my shotgun. I'll kill the big son-of-a-bitch myself. I'll shoot 'im in the guts[4]. Come on, you guys." He ran furiously out of the barn. Carlson said, "I'll get my Luger[5]," and he ran out too.

Slim turned quietly to George. "I guess Lennie done it, all right," he said. "Her neck's bust[6]. Lennie coulda did that."

George didn't answer, but he nodded[7] slowly. His hat was so far down on his forehead that his eyes were covered.

Slim went on, "Maybe like that time in Weed you was tellin' about."

Again George nodded.

Slim sighed. "Well, I guess we got to get him. Where you think he might of went?"

It seemed to take George some time to free his words. "He—would of went south," he said. "We come from north so he would of went south."

"I guess we gotta get 'im," Slim repeated.

George stepped close[8]. "Couldn' we maybe bring him in an' they'll lock him up? He's nuts, Slim. He never done this to be mean."

1. **crowded near** se rapprochèrent
2. **spell was broken** charme fut rompu
3. **worked himself** s'excita
4. **guts** ventre
5. **Luger** = pistol
6. **bust** pété
7. **nodded** acquiesça
8. **stepped close** se rapprocha

Slim nodded. "We might," he said. "If we could keep Curley in, we might. But Curley's gonna want to shoot 'im. Curley's still mad about his hand. An' s'pose they lock him up an' strap him down[1] and put him in a cage. That ain't no good, George."

"I know," said George. "I know."

Carlson came running in. "The bastard's stole my Luger," he shouted. "It ain't in my bag." Curley followed him, and Curley carried a shotgun in his good hand. Curley was cold now.

"All right, you guys," he said. "The nigger's got a shotgun. You take it, Carlson. When you see 'um, don't give 'im no chance. Shoot for his guts. That'll double 'im over[2]."

Whit said excitedly, "I ain't got a gun."

Curley said, "You go in Soledad an' get a cop[3]. Get Al Wilts, he's deputy sheriff. Le's go now." He turned suspiciously on George. "You're comin' with us, fella."

"Yeah," said George. "I'll come. But listen, Curley. The poor bastard's nuts. Don't shoot 'im. He di'n't know what he was doin'."

"Don't shoot 'im?" Curley cried. "He got Carlson's Luger. 'Course we'll shoot 'im."

George said weakly, "Maybe Carlson lost his gun."

"I seen it this morning," said Carlson. "No, it's been took[4]."

Slim stood looking down at Curley's wife. He said, "Curley—maybe you better stay here with your wife."

1. **strap him down** l'attachent

2. **that'll double 'im over** ça l'pliera en deux

3. **cop** flic

4. **took** = taken

Curley's face reddened[1]. "I'm goin'," he said. "I'm gonna shoot the guts outta that big bastard myself, even if I only got one hand. I'm gonna get 'im."

Slim turned to Candy. "You stay here with her then, Candy. The rest of us better get goin'."

They moved away. George stopped a moment beside Candy and they both looked down at the dead girl until Curley called, "You George! You stick[2] with us so we don't think you had nothin' to do with this."

2. **stick** restes

George moved slowly after them, and his feet dragged heavily[3].

3. **dragged heavily**
traînaient lourdement
4. **squatted down**
s'accroupit

And when they were gone, Candy squatted down[4] in the hay and watched the face of Curley's wife. "Poor bastard," he said softly.

5. **fainter** plus faible

The sound of the men grew fainter[5]. The barn was darkening gradually and, in their stalls, the horses shifted their feet and rattled the halter chains. Old Candy lay down in the hay and covered his eyes with his arm.

VI

PREVIOUSLY ON...

résumé
des épisodes
précédents

The deep green pool of the Salinas River was still in the late afternoon. Already the sun had left the valley to go climbing up[1] the slopes of the Gabilan mountains, and the hilltops were rosy[2] in the sun. But by the pool among the mottled[3] sycamores, a pleasant shade[4] had fallen.

A water snake glided smoothly[5] up the pool, twisting its periscope head from side to side; and it swam the length of the pool and came to the legs of a motionless heron that stood in the shallows[6]. A silent head and beak lanced down and plucked it out[7] by the head, and the beak swallowed[8] the little snake while its tail waved frantically[9].

A far rush of wind[10] sounded and a gust[11] drove through the tops of the trees like a wave. The sycamore leaves turned up their silver sides[12], the brown, dry leaves on the ground scudded[13] a few feet. And row on row[14] of tiny wind waves flowed up the pool's green surface.

As quickly as it had come, the wind died, and the clearing was quiet again. The heron stood in the shallows, motionless and waiting. Another little water snake swam up the pool, turning its periscope head from side to side.

Suddenly Lennie appeared out of the brush, and he came as silently as a creeping[15] bear moves. The heron pounded[16] the air with its wings, jacked itself clear[17] of the water and flew off down river. The little snake slid in among the reeds[18] at the pool's side.

1. **climbing up** escalader

2. **were rosy** prenaient une teinte rosée
3. **mottled** marbrès
4. **shade** ombre

5. **glided smoothly** glissait souplement

6. **the shallows** la partie peu profonde du bassin
7. **plucked it out** l'attrapa
8. **swallowed** avala

9. **waved frantically** battait furieusement
10. **rush of wind** coup de vent
11. **gust** bourrasque
12. **silver sides** faces argentées
13. **scudded** s'éparpillèrent

14. **row on row** une succession

15. **creeping** rampant

16. **pounded** battit
17. **jacked itself clear** se propulsa hors

18. **reeds** roseaux

Lennie came quietly to the pool's edge. He knelt down and drank, barely[1] touching his lips to the water. When a little bird skittered over[2] the dry leaves behind him, his head jerked up and he strained[3] toward the sound with eyes and ears until he saw the bird, and then he dropped his head and drank again.

When he finished, he sat down on the bank, with his side to the pool, so that he could watch the trail's entrance[4]. He embraced his knees and laid his chin down on his knees.

The light climbed on out of the valley, and as it went, the tops of the mountains seemed to blaze[5] with increasing brightness.

Lennie said softly, "I di'n't forget, you bet, God damn. Hide in the brush an' wait for George." He pulled his hat down low over his eyes. "George gonna give me hell," he said. "George gonna wish he was alone an' not have me botherin'[6] him." He turned his head and looked at the bright mountaintops. "I can go right off there an' find a cave[7]," he said. And he continued sadly, "—an' never have no ketchup—but I won't care. If George don't want me . . . I'll go away. I'll go away."

And then from out of Lennie's head there came a little fat old woman. She wore thick bull's-eye glasses[8] and she wore a huge gingham apron[9] with pockets, and she was starched[10] and clean. She stood in front of Lennie and put her hands on her hips, and she frowned disapprovingly at him.

1. **barely** à peine
2. **skittered over** sautilla par-dessus
3. **strained** se concentra
4. **the trail's entrance** l'arrivée du sentier
5. **blaze** s'embraser
6. **botherin'** qui l'ennuie
7. **cave** grotte
8. **thick bull's-eye glasses** des lunettes rondes à verres épais
9. **gingham apron** tablier à carreaux
10. **starched** empesée (les habits amidonnés, rigides)

1. **min'** = mind = listen to

2. **alla** = all the

3. **more'n** = more than
4. **they** = there

5. **coulda** = could have

6. **raised hell** fait la bringue
7. **snooker** variante du billard

8. **moaned with grief** gémissait de chagrin

9. **sonofabitching well** = damn well

10. **stew the b'Jesus outta** emmerder

And when she spoke, it was in Lennie's voice. "I tol' you an' tol' you," she said. "I tol' you, 'Min'[1] George because he's such a nice fella an' good to you.' But you don't never take no care. You do bad things."

And Lennie answered her, "I tried, Aunt Clara, ma'am. I tried and tried. I couldn' help it."

"You never give a thought to George," she went on in Lennie's voice. "He been doin' nice things for you alla[2] time. When he got a piece a pie you always got half or more'n[3] half. An' if they[4] was any ketchup, why he'd give it all to you."

"I know," said Lennie miserably. "I tried, Aunt Clara, ma'am. I tried and tried."

She interrupted him. "All the time he coulda[5] had such a good time if it wasn't for you. He woulda took his pay an' raised hell[6] in a whore house, and he coulda set in a poolroom an' played snooker[7]. But he got to take care of you."

Lennie moaned with grief[8]. "I know, Aunt Clara, ma'am. I'll go right off in the hills an' I'll fin' a cave an' I'll live there so I won't be no more trouble to George."

"You jus' say that," she said sharply. "You're always sayin' that, an' you know sonofabitching well[9] you ain't never gonna do it. You'll jus' stick around an' stew the b'Jesus outta[10] George all the time."

Lennie said, "I might jus' as well go away. George ain't gonna let me tend no rabbits now."

128

Aunt Clara was gone, and from out of Lennie's head there came a gigantic rabbit. It sat on its haunches[1] in front of him, and it waggled[2] its ears and crinkled[3] its nose at him. And it spoke in Lennie's voice too.

"Tend rabbits," it said scornfully[4]. "You crazy bastard. You ain't fit to lick the boots of no rabbit. You'd forget 'em and let 'em go hungry. That's what you'd do. An' then what would George think?"

"I would *not* forget," Lennie said loudly.

"The hell you wouldn'[5]," said the rabbit. "You ain't worth a greased jack-pin to ram you into hell[6]. Christ knows George done ever'thing he could to jack you outta the sewer[7], but it don't do no good. If you think George gonna let you tend rabbits, you're even crazier'n[8] usual. He ain't. He's gonna beat hell outta you with a stick, that's what he's gonna do."

Now Lennie retorted belligerently[9], "He ain't neither[10]. George won't do nothing like that. I've knew[11] George since—I forget when—and he ain't never raised his han'[12] to me with a stick. He's nice to me. He ain't gonna be mean."

"Well he's sick of you," said the rabbit. "He's gonna beat hell outta you an' then go away an' leave you."

"He won't," Lennie cried frantically. "He won't do nothing like that. I know George. Me an' him travels[13] together."

But the rabbit repeated softly over and over, "He gonna leave you, ya crazy bastard. He gonna leave ya all alone. He gonna leave ya, crazy bastard."

1. **haunches** pattes arrières
2. **waggled** agita
3. **crinkled** plissa
4. **scornfully** avec mépris
5. **the hell you wouldn'** = of course you would [forget]
6. **you ain't worth a greased jack-pin to ram you into hell** tu vaux même pas la corde pour te pendre
7. **jack you outta the sewer** te tirer du caniveau
8. **crazier'n** = crazier than
9. **retorted belligerently** répliqua hargneusement
10. **ain't neither** = won't
11. **knew** = known
12. **han'** = hand
13. **travels** = travel

Lennie put his hands over his ears. "He ain't, I tell ya he ain't." And he cried, "Oh! George—George—George!"

George came quietly out of the brush and the rabbit scuttled back[1] into Lennie's brain.

George said quietly, "What the hell you yellin'[2] about?"

Lennie got up on his knees. "You ain't gonna leave me, are ya, George? I know you ain't."

George came stiffly near and sat down beside him. "No."

"I knowed[3] it," Lennie cried. "You ain't that kind[4]."

George was silent.

Lennie said, "George."

"Yeah?"

"I done another bad thing."

"It don't make no difference," George said, and he fell silent again.

Only the topmost ridges[5] were in the sun now. The shadow in the valley was blue and soft. From the distance came the sound of men shouting to one another. George turned his head and listened to the shouts.

Lennie said, "George."

"Yeah?"

"Ain't you gonna give me hell?"

"Give ya hell?"

"Sure, like you always done before. Like, 'If I dis'n't[6] have you I'd take my fifty bucks——' "

"Jesus Christ, Lennie! You can't remember nothing that happens, but you remember ever' word I say."

1. **scuttled back** rentra se cacher
2. **yellin'** hurles
3. **knowed** = knew
4. **that kind** de ce genre
5. **the topmost ridges** les crêtes les plus hautes
6. **dis'n't** = didn't

"Well, ain't you gonna say it?"

George shook[1] himself. He said woodenly[2], "If I was alone I could live so easy." His voice was monotonous, had no emphasis. "I could get a job an' not have no mess." He stopped.

1. shook secoua
2. woodenly avec raideur

"Go on," said Lennie. "An' when the enda[3] the month come——"

3. enda = end of

"An' when the end of the month come I could take my fifty bucks an' go to a . . . cat house . . ." He stopped again.

Lennie looked eagerly[4] at him. "Go on, George. Ain't you gonna give me no more hell?"

4. eagerly avec impatience

"No," said George.

"Well, I can go away," said Lennie. "I'll go right off in the hills an' find a cave if you don' want me."

George shook himself again. "No," he said. "I want you to stay with me here."

Lennie said craftily[5]—"Tell me like you done before."

5. craftily avec astuce

"Tell you what?"

" 'Bout the other guys an' about us."

George said, "Guys like us got no family. They make a little stake[6] an' then they blow it in[7]. They ain't got nobody in the worl' that gives a hoot in hell[8] about 'em——"

6. a little stake = a little money
7. blow it in = spend it in
8. gives a hoot in hell en a quelque chose à faire

"*But not us*," Lennie cried happily. "Tell about us now."

George was quiet for a moment. "But not us," he said.

"Because——"

"Because I got you an'——"

"An' I got you. We got each other, that's what, that gives a hoot in hell about us," Lennie cried in triumph.

The little evening breeze blew over the clearing and the leaves rustled[1] and the wind waves flowed up the green pool. And the shouts of men sounded again, this time much closer than before.

George took off his hat. He said shakily[2], "Take off your hat, Lennie. The air feels fine[3]."

Lennie removed his hat dutifully[4] and laid it on the ground in front of him. The shadow in the valley was bluer, and the evening came fast[5]. On the wind the sound of crashing in the brush[6] came to them.

Lennie said, "Tell how it's gonna be."

George had been listening to the distant sounds. For a moment he was business-like. "Look acrost[7] the river, Lennie, an' I'll tell you so you can almost see it."

Lennie turned his head and looked off across the pool and up the darkening slopes of the Gabilans. "We gonna get a little place," George began. He reached in his side pocket and brought out Carlson's Luger; he snapped off the safety[8], and the hand and gun lay on the ground behind Lennie's back. He looked at the back of Lennie's head, at the place where the spine and skull[9] were joined.

A man's voice called from up the river, and another man answered.

"Go on," said Lennie.

George raised the gun and his hand shook[10], and he dropped his hand to the ground again.

1. **rustled** bruissaient

2. **shakily** d'une voix tremblante
3. **fine** = good

4. **dutifully** diligemment

5. **the evening came fast** le jour tombait rapidement
6. **crashing in the brush** brindilles écrasées

7. **acrost** = across

8. **snapped off the safety** enleva le cran d'arrêt

9. **the spine and skull** la colonne vertébrale et le crâne

10. **shook** trembla

"Go on," said Lennie. "How's it gonna be? We gonna get a little place."

"We'll have a cow," said George. "An' we'll have maybe a pig an' chickens . . . an' down the flat[1] we'll have a . . . little piece alfalfa—"

1. **flat** = field

"For the rabbits," Lennie shouted.

"For the rabbits," George repeated.

"And I get to tend the rabbits."

"An' you get to tend the rabbits."

Lennie giggled[2] with happiness. "An' live on the fatta the lan'."

2. **giggled** gloussa

"Yes."

Lennie turned his head.

"No, Lennie. Look down there acrost the river, like you can almost see the place."

Lennie obeyed him. George looked down at the gun.

There were crashing footsteps in the brush now. George turned and looked toward them.

"Go on, George. When we gonna do it?"

"Gonna do it soon."

"Me an' you."

"You . . . an' me. Ever'body gonna be nice to you. Ain't gonna be no more trouble. Nobody gonna hurt nobody nor steal from 'em."

Lennie said, "I thought you was mad at me, George."

"No," said George. "No, Lennie. I ain't mad. I never been mad, an' I ain't now. That's a thing I want ya to know."

1. **came close** se rapprochaient

2. **begged** supplia

3. **steadied it** le stabilisa

4. **muzzle** canon

5. **his face set** son visage se durcit
6. **pulled the trigger** tira

7. **jarred** eut un soubresaut
8. **settled slowly forward** s'affaissa doucement vers l'avant
9. **without quivering** sans un frémissement
10. **shivered** fut parcouru d'un frisson

11. **was ahead** était devant

12. **never you mind** = don't worry about it
13. **got to** = has to

The voices came close[1] now. George raised the gun and listened to the voices.

Lennie begged[2], "Le's do it now. Le's get that place now."

"Sure, right now. I gotta. We gotta."

And George raised the gun and steadied it[3], and he brought the muzzle[4] of it close to the back of Lennie's head. The hand shook violently, but his face set[5] and his hand steadied. He pulled the trigger[6]. The crash of the shot rolled up the hills and rolled down again. Lennie jarred[7], and then settled slowly forward[8] to the sand, and he lay without quivering[9].

George shivered[10] and looked at the gun, and then he threw it from him, back up on the bank, near the pile of old ashes.

The brush seemed filled with cries and with the sound of running feet. Slim's voice shouted, "George. Where you at, George?"

But George sat stiffly on the bank and looked at his right hand that had thrown the gun away. The group burst into the clearing, and Curley was ahead[11]. He saw Lennie lying on the sand. "Got him, by God." He went over and looked down at Lennie, and then he looked back at George. "Right in the back of the head," he said softly.

Slim came directly to George and sat down beside him, sat very close to him. "Never you mind[12]," said Slim. "A guy got to[13] sometimes."

But Carlson was standing over George. "How'd you do it?" he asked.

134

"I just done it," George said tiredly[1].

"Did he have my gun?"

"Yeah. He had your gun."

"An' you got it away from him and you took it an' you killed him?"

"Yeah. Tha's how." George's voice was almost a whisper[2]. He looked steadily at his right hand that had held the gun.

Slim twitched[3] George's elbow. "Come on, George. Me an' you'll go in an' get a drink."

George let himself be helped to his feet. "Yeah, a drink."

Slim said, "You hadda[4], George. I swear you hadda. Come on with me." He led George into the entrance of the trail and up toward the highway.

Curley and Carlson looked after them. And Carlson said, "Now what the hell ya suppose is eatin' them[5] two guys?"

1. **tiredly** d'un ton las

2. **whisper** murmure

3. **twitched** remua

4. **hadda** = had to

5. **eatin' them** les tracasse

Of Mice and Men

Title Of Mice and Men

Author John Steinbeck

Type of work Novella, 6 parts

Published in 1937, America

Genre Tragedy, social realism

Tone Serious, melancholic, fatalistic

Set in Rural California, 1930s

Spans over 4 days, Thursday to Sunday

Protagonists George and Lennie (migrant workers travelling together), Candy, Slim and Crooks (workers on a ranch), Curley (the ranch boss's son), Curley's wife

Themes Friendship, dreams, loneliness, injustice

Fun Facts

▶ *Of Mice and Men* was number 5 of the top 100 banned books of 2000-2009, as given by the American Library Association. The reason? Offensive and racist language. It's in good company – the number 1 for that decade was the Harry Potter series of books!

▶ The title comes from the poem To a Mouse by Robert Burns: "The best laid schemes o' mice an' men / Gang aft agley". Written in 1785 in Scottish English, this verse means "The most carefully prepared plans often go wrong".

▶ The character Lennie was based on someone Steinbeck actually knew. He told the New York Times, "Lennie was a real person. He's in an insane asylum in California right now. I worked alongside him for many weeks. He didn't kill a girl. He killed a ranch foreman."

▶ One of the early drafts was eaten by Steinbeck's dog, Toby. This meant that Steinbeck had lost many weeks of work. As he wrote in a letter to his editor, "Two months' work to do over… There was no other draft." Computers' automatic backups have their uses after all!

▶ Steinbeck described *Of Mice and Men*, as an 'experiment', a novella that was at the same time a script for a play. The stage version was first performed in October 1937, the same year the novella was published.

Who is John Steinbeck?

His life in 10 dates

1902 John Ernst Steinbeck Jr. is born in California, where most of his novels will be set. While at school, he spends his summers working on ranches and with migrant workers, experiences he will write about later.

1925 After studying English Literature at Stanford University, he leaves without a degree. He works on nearby farms during this time to support himself as he begins to write.

1929 Steinbeck's first novel, *Cup of Gold*, is published. It does not sell well. Steinbeck's first success will come with *Tortilla Flat* in 1935.

1930 He marries the first of three wives, Carol Henning. He attempts to start a manufacturing business with friends, but with no success.

1937 *Of Mice and Men* is published. The novella and play are both successful financially and widely praised from the very start.

1939 *The Grapes of Wrath* is published, often considered as Steinbeck's greatest work. Set in the Great Depression (1929-1939, the worst economic crisis in the history of the industrialized world) this novel wins the Pulitzer Prize for Fiction the following year.

1943 Steinbeck works as a war correspondent. During the war he receives physical injuries and also experiences psychological trauma.

1952 *East of Eden* is published. According to Steinbeck's third wife, Elaine Scott, he believes this to be his finest work.

1962 He wins the Nobel Prize in Literature. At the time this was controversial, with critics claiming he did not deserve the honor. The New York Times asked why the prize was given to a writer whose "limited talent is… watered down by tenth-rate philosophizing."

1968 On 20th December Steinbeck dies of heart failure aged 66, in New York City.

Why should we remember John Steinbeck?

Steinbeck is one of the most read and most loved of modern American authors. His greatest work, *The Grapes of Wrath*, has sold over 14 million copies and is considered one of the classics of American literature. In 2003's *The Big Read* in the UK, over 750,000 readers chose their favorite novels. *The Grapes of Wrath* was number 29 and *Of Mice and Men* came in at number 52, showing how well-loved these books remain.

The film versions of his works are also some of the great classics of cinema; in particular, 1952's *East of Eden*, starring James Dean in his first role. Steinbeck also wrote original screenplays, including *Viva Zapata!* (1952), for which he was nominated for an Oscar.

Of Mice and Men is set in rural California during the 1930s. This was the time of the **Great Depression**, a time of huge economic difficulty in America and around the world. This began with the **Wall Street Crash** of 1929 and only ended with the beginning of World War II. At the same time, bad weather was also hurting the agriculture sector, especially in the **Dust Bowl** (Southern Plains region of the United States, which suffered from heat and **dust storms** during a dry period in the 1930s).

Causes of the Great Depression

The **Great Depression** has a clear starting date: October 1929, the date of the **Wall Street Crash**. Over two days, the stock exchange fell around 23%, causing panic in America and abroad. The value of the stock market kept falling for many years, with shares losing almost 90% of their value.

The precise reasons for the Great Depression are still in dispute. Some believe the crash was in response to the **'Roaring Twenties,** the fast economic growth of America during the 1920s post WWI. After growing too fast for too long, this was a natural 'correction' to the economy. Others believe that the initial stock market crash caused people to save money and stop spending, in turn causing the economy to collapse. Yet another group believe the cause was a lack of money in circulation, caused by failing banks and insufficient government action.

Effects of the Great Depression

Around 13 million people became unemployed in America, with a 24.9% unemployment rate, and the income of the average family fell by 40%. 11,000 banks failed, with 9 million savings accounts becoming worthless. This was the greatest economic disaster in the history of the developed world.

Prices fell, with food prices going so low that many farmers went bankrupt. This was partly due to farmers producing too much food. The low prices pushed many farmers to try to produce even more, replacing grassland with more crops. At one point, the price of corn fell lower than coal. In some places the countryside smelled like popcorn from all the corn burning in kitchen stoves.

Migration and the Dust Bowl

There was severe **drought** in the **Dust Bowl** area of America in 1930s, centered in Oklahoma but also affecting states like Colorado, Kansas, Texas, New Mexico and the south of Nebraska. In these areas the prairie grass, with long roots, had previously kept the soil in place. Too much plowing and farming now left the soil in poor condition. Lack of rain turned the soil to dust, leading to **dust storms** that blew much of the precious topsoil away. These dust storms were so thick they darkened the sky, turning day into night.

By 1934, over 1 million families had lost their farms. Around 2.5 million people moved away from the Dust Bowl states, with over 250,000 moving from Oklahoma to California. The difficult lives of these 'Okies' is described in Steinbeck's *The Grapes of Wrath*.

California, the setting for *Of Mice and Men*, also suffered from droughts and the effects of the Great Depression. Many local farmers lost their farms and many farmhands and factory workers were laid off. Over 500,000 Mexican Americans were deported or pushed to return to Mexico, as workers with 'American' names were favored.

The struggle of the disadvantaged

Steinbeck's novella focuses on the **working class**, poor people with few rights or opportunities for the future, and looks into the lives of different groups of disadvantaged people. Curley's wife shows some of the problems that **women** had at the time. Crooks, the black stable-buck, is an example of the difficult situation **black people** were in. Together, Lennie and Candy show the limited choices available to the **mentally and physically disabled**.

Some workers did band together to fight for better conditions, but strikes and other protests were often violently broken up. When the economy started suffering, millions were laid off. Factories and farms used this opportunity to reduce wages, knowing that workers would be too afraid to leave, as jobs were rare. Workers had no

choice but to accept what little they were given.

Non-whites were in an even worse situation. Between 1929 and 1936 it is estimated that up to two million Mexicans and Mexican Americans were deported to Mexico, including perhaps a million American citizens. This was to protect "American jobs". **Black people** were second class citizens, especially in southern states. They were often fired before white workers and were less likely to be given jobs. Public assistance programs of the time, meant to help the poorest, sometimes refused aid to black people.

The **disabled** encountered even greater problems. There were few jobs available for disabled workers and little financial help from the government. Those who were injured at work could expect little compensation. In *Of Mice and Men*, Candy is given $250 for the loss of a hand at work, a sum equal to only five months' wages. The mentally disabled of this time were usually put into special institutions. They were often given heavy doses of drugs and lived in very poor conditions.

Women also suffered badly in this time. Male workers joining the fighting in World War I had opened up positions for women to work. After the war ended, many of these women continued to work. However, the Great Depression reduced the need for workers and many employers preferred to hire men. This greatly reduced the opportunities open to women. For many girls, this left only one possible path in life: marrying a man and having children.

How does it all begin?

Two workers, George and Lennie, are travelling to a ranch to work. Lennie is an innocent and simpleminded giant, physically very strong, but mentally childlike. He relies on George to look after him. As they travel, Lennie plays with a dead mouse he had accidentally killed earlier. When they arrive on the ranch, they meet the boss and some workers. Curley, the boss's son, an ill-tempered bully, dislikes the two new men…

What happens next?

George and Lennie often talk about their longstanding dream of having their own farm. Crooks and Candy, two workers on the farm, want to join them in their plan. Meanwhile, Curley's provocative new wife is causing trouble for Curley, which makes him angry. He picks a fight with Lennie, who protects himself and badly injures Curley's hand in the process…

What's the climax of the story?

Lennie goes to the barn to play with a puppy he has been given. Curley's wife goes to talk with him and lets him stroke her hair. She gets upset and he tries to keep her quiet, but he is so strong he accidentally breaks her neck. He remembers George told him that if there was trouble, they should meet by the riverside near the ranch. After he leaves, the other men find her body and decide to hunt Lennie down…

Spoiler alert!

How does it end?

Lennie goes to the riverside and waits for George. When George arrives, he tells Lennie that everything is fine and describes once again the wonderful dream they have. George knows that if Lennie lives, he'll be sent to prison or badly hurt. As Lennie happily imagines the future, George shoots his friend in the back of the head.

Characters

George Milton
A small, quick, uneducated yet intelligent man

He is trying to survive in a difficult time and at the same time look after his friend Lennie. He has had to save Lennie many times in the past, but still stays with him, showing his loyalty and need for companionship.

Lennie Small
A very large and strong man, but with the mind of a child

He relies on George for everything, but his strength and mental disability often cause problems. His dream is to live with George on their own farm, with pet rabbits he can play with.

Candy
An old ranch worker

Candy lost one of his hands working on the ranch. Now he has the lowly job of keeping the accommodation clean. He is worried that he will lose his job and be unable to find another.

Slim
A leader amongst the ranch workers

As a jerkline skinner (the leader of a team of mules), Slim has one of the most important positions on the ranch. He is very well respected by all those who know him for his knowledge, wisdom, and experience.

Crooks
A black stable buck

He looks after the horses. His color sets him apart and forces him to live separately from the other men on the ranch. He is crippled, with a bent spine.

Curley
The son of the ranch's boss

He is a small man with a dislike of bigger men. He is proud of his power on the ranch and protective of his wife, who he has only recently married.

Curley's wife
A young, pretty and flirtatious girl

She seems disappointed with her new husband and often looks back to opportunities she had in the past. She is the only character not given a name in the book.

We can understand the characters in *Of Mice and Men* better if we look at the words associated with them the most in the novel.

Lennie

• Rabbits

Lennie dreams about looking after some **rabbits** on the land he and George hope to buy. They are his primary concern and the embodiment of his dreams: in the end, Lennie's visions actually take the form of a giant rabbit, showing how important they are in his mind.

• Hands

Lennie's **'big hands'** or **'big paws'** represent his incredible physical strength, a strength he doesn't control. However, despite being so strong, Lennie is often portrayed as defenceless, like a baby, when it comes to dangerous situations.

*"Lennie covered his face with his **huge paws** and bleated with terror."*

Even though Lennie doesn't intend to hurt anything or anyone, his powerful **hands** are deadly for the mice, his pup, and ultimately Curley's wife.

• Bad things

Lennie likes to pet little furry animals and touch hair and soft cloth but when he gets excited, he accidentally does harm to others. Lennie understands these negative consequences of his behaviour as **'bad things.'**

*"When she didn't answer nor move, he bent closely over her. He lifted her arm and let it drop. For a moment he seemed bewildered. And then he whispered in fright, 'I done a bad thing. I done another **bad thing.**'"*

Candy

• Old

One of the first adjectives used to describe Candy is 'old.' He is living out his later years on the ranch, struggling to work because he lost his arm in an accident. This makes him worry that the boss will eventually ask him to leave.

"Old Candy, the swamper, came in and went to his bunk, and behind him struggled his old dog."

• Stump

Candy's **stump** is what's left of his arm after his accident, where he lost his hand. You will often see Candy being described as repeatedly rubbing or scratching his wrist stump. In the same way that hands in *Of Mice and Men* symbolize a man's moral and physical strength, Candy's stump represents his helplessness. In a world without compassion, what happens to an old handyman who's lost a hand?

• Dog

Just like Candy, his **dog** is old and frail. It cannot perform its role as sheepdog on the ranch anymore. The dog represents Candy's fears of becoming useless and replaceable. Carlson, another worker on the farm, insists on shooting the dog dead. Candy later regrets this choice, wishing he had done it himself, as he felt it was his responsibility. The death of Candy's old dog symbolizes the tragic and hopeless fate of those who are no longer 'useful' in this society.

*"You seen what they done to my **dog** tonight? They says he wasn't no good to himself nor nobody else. When they can me here I wisht somebody'd shoot me. But they won't do nothing like that. I won't have no place to go, an' I can't get no more jobs."*

Curley's wife

• Curley

The one woman that we are introduced to in the novel is described only as '**Curley**'s wife': we don't even get to know her real name. She only exists in relation to her husband, as her individual sense of identity doesn't matter in this world.

• Eye

One of the first things that we learn about Curley's wife is that '**she got the eye**', meaning that she enjoys flirting with other men. It also highlights the fact that she seems to only exist in the eyes of men: the jealous **eyes** of her husband, the lustful yet scornful eyes of the other workers on the ranch, none of whom really respect her or acknowledge her as a proper individual.

"Yeah. Purty... but—" George studied his cards. "But what?" "Well–she got the eye." "Yeah? Married two weeks and got the eye?"

Slim

• Authority

Slim is a jerkline skinner, the lead driver of a team of mules. Contrary to Curley, the boss's son, he commands **authority** not because he is necessarily stronger or richer than the others, but because he is described as a natural leader. He is 'the prince of the ranch', moving 'with a majesty only achieved by royalty and master craftsmen' and his words are law.

*"Candy looked helplessly at him, for Slim's opinions were **law**."*

• Calm & Friendly

Slim is different from the other ranch men: he is a **calm** and wise figure, and his actions and physical traits are often described with adjectives that reflect his peaceful personality. His voice is 'gentle' and '**friendly**', his actions throughout the story are 'slow', which suggests he reflects before acting, and his eyes are 'calm, Godlike'.

George

• Bindle

George and Lennie are **bindlestiffs** (travelers or migrant workers). They wander around America looking for work on ranches, carrying their few possessions inside a blanket tied up to the end of a stick over their shoulders, called a **bindle**.

When they get to the ranch, George unrolls his bindle, takes his razor and soap out of it, and puts them on a shelf. This shows that they are going to settle down, and stop travelling, for a while at least.

*"I seen hunderds of men come by on the road an' on the ranches, with their **bindles** on their back an' that same damn thing in their heads. Hunderds of them. They come, an' they quit an' go on; an' every damn one of 'em's got a little piece of land in his head."*

• Bastard

George often addresses, or speaks of Lennie as a **poor bastard** or a **crazy bastard**, and Lennie himself, when he gets to the riverbank where he is supposed to hide, addresses himself in the same way, voicing his fear that George is going to leave him:

*"He gonna leave you, ya crazy **bastard**. He gonna leave ya all alone."*

It's an offensive word, but George uses it affectionately. By using the word, he is almost acknowledging his friend's faults, while also implying that he cares deeply for him.

• Getting canned

George fantasizes about a place where he and Lennie would belong, where they could work and live freely. As "bindlestiffs", or itinerant workers, their job is their only anchor: they have no house to return to, no life outside the ranch they work on. This also explains why **getting canned** is such a huge deal for them: no work means no life.

*"An' it'd be our own, an' nobody could **can** us."*

Crooks

• Buck

Crooks is an African American man who works in the stables at the ranch; he is named this way because of his crooked back, caused by a kick from a horse. Steinbeck describes him as a **stable buck**; this is a pejorative term used to describe black men who work in the stables. Incidentally, 'buck' can also mean 'dollar', as in 'fifty bucks'.

• Books

Crooks is not allowed to share the bunk house with his fellow ranchers because he is black. Thus, his only option is to read **books** to try and pass the time; but this still doesn't compare to human interaction:

*"S'pose you didn't have nobody. S'pose you couldn't go into the bunk house and play rummy 'cause you was black. How'd you like that? S'pose you had to sit out here an' read **books**. [...] **Books** ain't no good. A guy needs somebody–to be near him."*

Curley

• Little guy

Curley is a **little guy**. A feeling of inferiority makes him aggressive, arrogant and cruel. He is always agitated and tense, as his actions reveal: he bursts into rooms, glares at people and gets angry easily.

*"Curley's like a lot of **little guys**. He hates big guys. He's alla time picking scraps with big guys. Kind of like he's mad at 'em because he ain't a big guy."*

• Handy

Curley is often described as **handy**, someone who's good at fighting with his hands. He constantly tries to assert his superiority by getting into fights. He is a bully who tries to compensate for being small by being hostile and mean. On the other end of the spectrum, Lennie is big and has big hands, but doesn't want to fight, and doesn't know how.

*"Curley's just spoilin' or he wouldn't start for Slim. An' Curley's **handy**, God damn handy."*

Steinbeck's American English

Many characters in the book are shown speaking non-standard English.
This is partly used as a way for Steinbeck to show their accents and the language of the time. It is also a sign that they have received very little formal education.

Here are some examples of non-standard English that can be seen throughout the novella.

- **The first and final sound of many words is missed.**

talking	⟹ talkin'
just	⟹ jes'
spend	⟹ spen'
all of the	⟹ alla

raccoon	⟹ 'coon
them	⟹ 'em
because	⟹ 'cause
instead	⟹ 'stead

- **The simple words 'to', 'of' and 'have' are added to the previous word.**

want to	⟹ wanta, wanna
out of	⟹ outa
must have	⟹ musta
full of	⟹ fulla
couple of	⟹ coupla
kind of	⟹ kinda
ought to	⟹ oughta
used to	⟹ usta
had to	⟹ hadda

- **The use of non-standard tenses to talk about the past.**

Well, I never **seen** one guy take so much trouble for another guy.
⟹ Well, **I have never seen...**

I **knew** his Aunt Clara. ⟹ I **knowed** his Aunt Clara.

150

• Past simple ending in -t.

Some verbs in the past simple tense appear ending in -t instead of -ed. Here are some examples:

scar**ed** ➡ sca**irt**

wish ➡ wish**t**

ask**ed** ➡ ast

• Two negative words when only one should be used.

"Don't tell nobody"

"They won't do nothing like that"

"I ain't no good at it"

• Using 'was' for 'were' and 'don't' for 'doesn't'.

"We was eatin'"

"Chickens they was"

"She don't care"

"He don't like nobody"

• Some words are spelt as they are pronounced by the characters.

across ➡ acrost

you ➡ ya

all right ➡ awright

pretty ➡ purty

• There are also many words and expression that are not common in modern English, like:

bindle	➡ a bundle of clothes or bedding
bindle stiff	➡ a traveling worker or homeless person, carrying a bindle
to buck	➡ to throw into a truck or wagon
to get the can	➡ to be fired
jack	➡ money
swamper	➡ a cleaner
stable buck	➡ the lowest job in a stable
jerkline skinner	➡ the driver of a mule train

Male friendship

Friendships and interactions between the male characters are shown in different ways. For most of the workers on the ranch, being laborers in the **Great Depression** means that they live a **precarious** life. The workers on the ranch know that their colleagues might leave soon and so are unwilling to work on "real" friendships. We are shown many brief insights into the lives of previous workers on the ranch and the limited connections they made while they were there.

The friendship between George and Lennie is at the heart of the story. We are given little information about why the two men are together, but it is clear that they have been together for some time and have a deep relationship. For Lennie, this friendship is **simple and pure**. He loves George, trusts him and can hardly imagine life without his friend. For George, their relationship is more complex. He regards Lennie as a **responsibility** and sometimes as a **burden**. However, he also feels strongly for his friend and closely **values his companionship**, without which he would be alone in the world. He

> The friendship between George and Lennie is at the heart of the story.

also knows that his duty to Lennie and the sense of **brotherhood** it brings make him a better man.

Even so, it is stressed several times that this kind of relationship is **rare**. Slim, looking at the two men, wonders why that is, concluding that **loneliness is a vicious cycle** that separates men because they end up **scared** of each other. The boss of the ranch thinks their friendship is so unusual that it must be **suspicious**, and he assumes George must be taking advantage of Lennie. In the eyes of the majority, their friendship, just like their dream, is **too good to be true**.

Power, or the lack thereof, also influences each character's attitude to friendship. The two weakest men on the ranch, Candy and Crooks, are both willing to team up to buy the farm, a sign that George and Lennie have something valuable together. Curley, who is more powerful as he is the boss's son, does not seem to regard friendship with the ranch workers as either necessary or even desirable.

Loneliness

Loneliness, the opposite of friendship, is perhaps an even more important theme in the book. Almost every character of *Of Mice and Men* is lonely or separated from the others in some way. Crooks is the clearest example of this. As the only **black man** on the ranch, he lives alone and is apart from the other men. When Lennie and Candy enter his home, he is secretly happy to have new people come to see him.

> Almost every character of *Of Mice and Men* is lonely or separated from the others in some way.

Candy is the least powerful of the white workers on the ranch and is **worried for the future**. The other men **pressure** him to allow his dog to be killed, separating him from the strongest attachment he has to another living thing. He regards **loneliness as natural**, saying "*A guy on a ranch don't never listen nor he don't ast no questions.*"

Curley's wife is lonely for other reasons. She is a newly married wife, but **regrets marrying** Curley and yearns for more. She tries to talk to the other men on the ranch, but they are unwilling to be seen with her, or are worried she will get them in trouble.

Soledad, the city next to the ranch, literally means loneliness in Spanish, which is quite fitting as the workers go there to seek out the company of ladies in cat-houses, spending their money on **fruitless relationships**, coming back to the ranch as lonely as ever.

The dangers of loneliness are also discussed several times. Crooks says that if someone is truly alone, they will go **crazy**. George states that he sees what happens to men that travel around on their own: "*I seen the guys that go around on the ranches alone. That ain't no good. They don't have no fun. After a long time they get mean.*" This may be the future he is looking at for himself at the end of the story, which shows the darker and **fatalistic undertone** of the novel.

Dreams for the future

George and Lennie's dream of being independent landowners is central to the plot, and also to the two men themselves. This **long-term dream** is shown as a distant vision at the start of the story. Then, when Candy offers his money to help, it seems the dream may be about to come true. Later it is shown to be something that was always **impossible**, a story to keep Lennie (and George himself) happy and provide them with a **purpose**, a reason to keep going.

Candy and Crooks, **marginalized** characters, are also willing to join the dream. Candy really believes it might happen, and that there is an actual future for him, where he can live a comfortable life. Crooks is more **realistic**. He allows himself to believe only for a few minutes. Then his natural **pessimism**, born from years of abuse for being a poor black man and a cripple, tells him the truth

> George and Lennie's dream of being independent landowners is central to the plot.

that it will never happen, and he ends up being right.

Curley's wife talks about the dreams **she used to have**. She believes she could have been an actress. She compares her dreams of nice clothes and big hotels with her current life. She seems to think that life as a successful actress was a real possibility, though it is not clear whether there was ever any chance of this becoming true. It makes her character all the more **tragic**.

Dreams are such a central theme that at the end of the novella, Lennie imagines his dream **come to life**. He sees a giant rabbit appear before him, though only to **curse** him for his actions and **threaten** that George will leave him. This rabbit, representing Lennie's dreams for the future, tells him that those are now **gone forever**.

Lack of power

The characters are often shown as having no choices and no other options than going on with their lives the way they already are. This lack of power comes from many sources. The main characters in the novella are the lowest-level workers on the farm. They are all **poor**, in a **depression economy** where jobs are scarce. They **lack the skills or the education** to lift themselves to a better position.

Crooks is the most obvious example of this **lack of power**. As a **disabled** black man, he is the least important worker on the ranch. He is proud of what he has, but knows that he is under the control of others. As Curley's wife tells him, "*I could get you strung up on a tree so easy it ain't even funny.*"

But even though most of the workers lack power, Candy is the one who appears to

> The characters are often shown as having no choices and no other options than going on with their lives the way they already are.

be in the **weakest** position. Having lost a hand, he knows he can't find another job. He can only stay on the ranch, waiting until they decide that it's not worth keeping him around. Candy's **powerlessness** is such that he can't even stop the other workers from **killing his beloved dog**. The fate of his pet reflects what could happen to him, which explains why he is so **desperate** to make George and Lennie's dream come true.

Another kind of **powerlessness** is portrayed in George's decision to shoot Lennie at the end of the novel. Despite his love for his friend, he **cannot see another solution** to the problem, as Lennie could not survive alone or in prison. Slim shows he agrees with George that there was no other choice, saying: "*You hadda, George. I swear you hadda.*".

1 It is a significant part of American culture

Of Mice and Men has been filmed four times in America and adaptations of the story have been made in Iran and India. There have also been many successful stage performances and even an opera based on the story. Many movies, cartoons and books have referenced the relationship between Lennie and George, so you might meet these characters again!

2 It is very popular and has universal themes

Over 90% of British students study *Of Mice and Men* at school and it is commonly studied throughout the English-speaking world. One reason for this choice (apart from its being quite short!) is the compassion that is portrayed in the novella. Many schools use the story to help students learn about and combat bullying, examining how Lennie, Crooks and Candy are mistreated for being different.

3 It is a revealing insight into the Great Depression

Steinbeck's *Of Mice and Men* and *The Grapes of Wrath* are the two novels that most represent the Great Depression and the lives of farmworkers during this time. For many people, these novels are their central source of information on the lives of the working class during the 1930s, and they can help us learn about this challenging time.

> *Maybe ever'body in the whole damn world is scared of each other.*

Slim, thinking about why most men travel alone. (p. 46)

This quote explains why meeting new people and making new friends can be difficult; it suggests that relationships are rare and precious things.

How to use it
When you go to a party and don't feel welcome.

> *I got you to look after me, and you got me to look after you, and that's why.*

Lennie, explaining why he and George are going to have a great future together. (p. 20)

A simple way to describe how important friends and family are to each other. We don't have to explain it, it's just a simple truth.

How to use it
When you want to make an important person in your life feel special.

> *I tell ya a guy gets too lonely an' he gets sick.*

Crooks, complaining that, unlike Lennie, he has nobody he can count on. (p. 93)

This is another quote showing the importance of being around others. It's important to have people you can rely on, so that you don't become isolated or lonely.

How to use it
When your brother locks his bedroom door and won't come out.

Critics' reviews

Vast sense of compassion

"You will close this strange, tragic little idyll with a vast sense of compassion for big, dumb Lennie and for George, who knew Lennie would never get to tend those rabbits…"

Lewis Gannett book review in the New York Herald Tribune, February 1937

Stark little tragedy

"The apparent simplicity of this stark little tragedy … belies the magnitude and complexity of the moral questions it raises."

Marilyn Chandler McEntire, from *Cain Sign: The Betrayal of Brotherhood in The Work of John Steinbeck*, 2000

Dream of breathless beauty

"*Of Mice and Men* by John Steinbeck is a book so powerful it will make the reader's hair stand on end … however, beneath the superficial horror of the story the reader senses a dream of breathless beauty shimmering through the lives of the two main characters."

Maxine Garrard book review in the *Columbus Enquirer*, March 1937.

The first book I read that made me cry

"…it was the first book I read that made me cry. It has a sad, horrific ending, but exactly the right one. It was incredibly emotional, gritty and real, and it stayed with me all these years later. Over 30 years since I read it for the first time, and I still remember the vivid experience."

Damon Lindelof, creator of the TV shows 'Lost' and 'Watchmen', in an interview with HBO, 2020

Readers' reviews

Subtly and vividly portrayed Before you finish the first page you realize that you're reading an authentic poetic piece of literature. As with other John Steinbeck works, his recognition and homage to hard economic times in America, and the transient workforce is so subtly and vividly portrayed.

Peter,

Matchless expertise This short little novella packs a heavy punch to the readers' consciousness. Steinbeck is a writer who depicts the human psyche with a matchless expertise. The story is contemporary of the Great Depression of 30s, but the emotional characteristics of the book are timeless.

Abhishek Debnath,

Incredibly depressing! What a depressing story. Beautifully descriptive, but incredibly depressing. Life is too short for depressing fiction.

Sean Taylor,

A total embarrassment As soon as I opened the book and read the first page, I knew that there wasn't going to be enough pages to carry on with an interesting plot. As I got to about page 5 and read about the characters, I realized that they were extremely predictable and see-through… This book is a total embarrassment to American literature and a waste of trees.

Amazing Reviewer,

What side are you on?

What did you think of *Of Mice and Men?*

Quiz & Recap

Quiz

1 **How is George described at the beginning of the chapter?**
Pick four out of the following words and phrases.   *4 pts*

| dark | huge | quick | thin | strong hands |

| wide shoulders | shapeless face |

2 **Why are the men travelling?**   *2 pts*

ⓐ They are going home after finishing a job.

ⓑ They are going to a farm where they have a job.

ⓒ They are walking around, looking for a job.

3 **When the two men have their own farm, they will...**   *2 pts*

ⓐ ...live off the fat of the land.

ⓑ ...live off the fruit of the earth.

ⓒ ...live off the food of the farm.

4 **What animals does Lennie want to play with on the farm?**   *2 pts*

ⓐ Chickens

ⓑ Mice

ⓒ Rabbits

1. dark, strong hands, quick, thin 2. b 3. a 4. c

Your score
...../10 pts

Recap

When?	Thursday evening
Where?	On the bank of the Salinas River, California
Who?	• George • Lennie
What?	George and Lennie are on the way to a ranch, where they have found a job. George decides to stop by a river and sleep there for the night, rather than go to the ranch immediately. George gets angry with Lennie as he keeps playing with a dead mouse. He complains about needing to look after Lennie and all the trouble Lennie causes for him. However, he soon calms down and tells Lennie that he is happy they are together. George talks about the events in Weed, where they had to run away after Lennie tried to touch a girl's dress. He tells Lennie that if something like that happens again, he should come back to the riverbank and hide. They both talk about their dream of having their own farm one day, where George can be his own boss and Lennie can play with the animals.

Key ideas

▷ **Trouble**

- George complains about having to look after Lennie. We learn about Lennie causing problems, forgetting things and accidentally killing small animals. They also discuss the events in Weed, where they were chased out of town after Lennie touched a girl's dress.
- It is implied that these problems have happened many times. George says, "You keep me in hot water all the time."

▷ **Friendship and loyalty**

- Despite the problems, we learn how the two men interact with each other, look after and help each other. They seem to share a strong bond, even if they're not related.
- George can be aggressive and controlling, but we learn that he forgives Lennie and looks after him. He seems to always help and resolve the problems that Lennie gets himself into.

▷ **Dreams**

- Their dream is mentioned for the first time, of a perfect future on their own farm. This will be a key idea, that is a leitmotif throughout the story.

Quiz

1 Match the characters to their jobs. *4 pts*

Curley **1**   **a** A 'jerkline skinner', a leader's role

Slim **2**   **b** A ranch worker

Candy **3**   **c** The boss's son

Carlson **4**   **d** The cleaner of the bunk house

2 What is Curley's wife's name? *2 pts*

a Clara.

b Murray.

c We don't know.

3 Curley's wife is said to give people 'the eye'. What does this mean? *2 pts*

a She flirts with them.

b She's watching them.

c She's suspicious of them.

4 Curley is described as 'pretty handy'. What does 'handy' mean here? *2 pts*

a He is useful around the ranch.

b He is good at fighting.

c He sometimes steals things.

1. 1=c, 2=a, 3=d, 4=b 2. c 3. a 4. b

Recap

When?	Friday morning
Where?	The bunk house, where the workers on the ranch sleep
Who?	• George • Lennie • the boss of the ranch and his son Curley • Curley's wife • workers on the ranch: Candy, Slim and Carlson
What?	George and Lennie arrive at the ranch and meet the boss, who signs them up as workers. They also meet Candy and his old, weak dog. Candy tries to make friends with George. Curley, the boss's son meets Lennie and George. He seems to dislike George and later Candy says he likes to pick fights with bigger men like Lennie. Curley's wife appears in the bunk house. George thinks her seductive looks make her dangerous, but Lennie thinks she's pretty. Carlson suggests killing Candy's dog and giving him one of Slim's dog's puppies. Lennie also wants a puppy and George agrees to ask Slim for one.

Key ideas

▷ **Introductions to the characters on the ranch**
- **Candy**, an old worker who is missing a hand. He can only work as a cleaner and is always followed by his old dog.
- **Curley**, the arrogant son of the boss. We learn he is a small man, with a habit of picking fights with larger men.
- **Curley's wife**, married for only two weeks. She is a pretty girl but has a reputation for being interested in other men.
- **Slim**, the top worker on the ranch. He is a confident, friendly and well-respected man who is happy to see the two new workers.
- **Carlson**, another worker, who brings up the suggestion of putting Candy's dog down.

▷ **Male interactions and suspicions**
- The boss talks to George, suspecting that his control over Lennie might be for George's own benefit.
- Curley and George meet, both immediately disliking the other.
- Candy and George are suspicious of each other at first, but Candy tries to make friends with George by telling him unpleasant information about Curley.
- The way Slim meets the two new men is different. He is the only person to talk to them in a completely positive way.

Quiz

1 George tells Slim about a joke he once played on Lennie. What was it? *2 pts*

  ⓐ He told him to jump off a cliff.

  ⓑ He told him to fight a man.

  ⓒ He told him to jump in a river.

2 Why is Carlson so keen to get rid of Candy's dog? *2 pts*

  ⓐ It bit him.

  ⓑ It smells bad.

  ⓒ He doesn't like dogs.

3 Link Lennie's actions with what happens next. *4 pts*

He brings a puppy into the bunk house. **❶**   **ⓐ** Curley gets angry with him.

He talks with George about their plan. **❷**   **ⓑ** Candy wants to join in.

He laughs in front of the other men. **❸**   **ⓒ** Curley's hand is crushed.

He gets into a fight. **❹**   **ⓓ** George gets angry with him.

4 Why won't Curley tell other people that Lennie hurt his hand? *2 pts*

  ⓐ He is afraid that other people will laugh at him.

  ⓑ He is afraid that Lennie will hurt him again.

  ⓒ He is afraid that Slim might hurt him.

1. c 2. b 3. 1=d, 2=b, 3=a, 4=c 4. a

Recap

When?	Friday evening
Where?	The bunk house
Who?	• George • Lennie • Curley • Curley's wife • Candy, Slim and Carlson • Crooks, a black man who looks after the horses • Whit, another worker
What?	Lennie gets one of the puppies. Candy agrees to let Carlson shoot his dog. George and Lennie talk about their dream again. Candy listens and asks to join in, offering his money to help make it happen. Curley comes in, looking for his wife. The other men laugh at him and he starts a fight with Lennie, who crushes Curley's hand defending himself. Slim tells Curley not to talk about this, or everyone will laugh at him.

Key ideas

▶ **Life on the ranch**
  • We learn about everyday life on the ranch and the way the men live and work together.
  • The men seem to live for the present, gambling away their money or spending it on alcohol and trips to a whorehouse. It is suggested they are doing jobs with no future, working for the long-term benefits of others.
  • We see strangers examining each other, testing each other and starting to make friends. This is shown as a natural but difficult process, and an important part of life on the ranch.

▶ **Loneliness and desperation**
  • Candy's dog is too old to be useful on the ranch. Candy wants someone to help him keep his dog, but no one does. Despite Candy's love for his old pet, he agrees that it should be shot. Old and with only one hand, Candy knows he may be kicked out one day and won't find another job. He sees his own life as little more valuable than that of his dog.

Quiz

1 In which order do the four people enter Crook's room? *3 pts*

   a Candy

   b Curley's wife

   c Lennie

   d George

2 Why does Crooks say, "Nobody never gets to heaven and nobody gets no land"? *2 pts*

   a He is saying that people like him and Lennie never achieve their dreams.

   b He is saying that black people will never be equal.

   c He is saying that he does not believe in God.

3 Match the phrases to their meanings. *3 pts*

   roll your hoop **1**   **a** lose your job

   get canned **2**   **b** go play a game

   get it coming **3**   **c** deserve it

4 Curley's wife says she's talking to "a nigger an' a dum-dum and a lousy ol' sheep." Who are these, in order? *2 pts*

   a Crooks, Lennie and Candy.

   b Crooks, Candy and Lennie.

   c Candy, Crooks and Lennie.

1. c a b d 2. a 3. 1=b, 2=a, 3=c 4. a

Your score
...../10 pts

Recap

When?	Saturday night
Where?	The harness room, where Crooks lives
Who?	• Crooks, the black stable worker • Lennie • Candy • Curley's wife • George
What?	Most of the workers have gone to town. Only Lennie, Crooks, Candy and Curley's wife remain at the ranch. Lennie comes to the harness room, where Crooks lives alone. Lennie tells Crooks about George and his dream for the future. Crooks begins by laughing at it, then wants to join, and finally rejects it, saying it will never happen. Candy and then Curley's wife come to the room. The men try to make her leave, but then she threatens Crooks and forces him to back down. She says that she knows Lennie is the one who hurt her husband's hand and leaves, just before the other men return.

Key ideas

▶ **Loneliness**

- Crooks lives alone, apart from the other men. It is clear that it is very unusual for the other men to enter his room. However, despite pretending to be annoyed, he is happy the other men visit him.
- A bit jealous of Lennie and George's friendship, he teases Lennie, pretending that George has gone, leaving Lennie alone.
- Crooks too is attracted by the idea of joining the other men in their dream and having a future together. Despite trying to appear aloof and happy to be apart, he shows he is also lonely and afraid of rejection.

▶ **Racism**

- Crooks is alone because he is black. This is presented as natural, a sign of how deep and widespread racism is at this time. Indeed, even though slavery has been abolished with the Civil War in 1865, racism is still very present, especially in rural America.
- Crooks is nonetheless proud of who he is. He has his own space and is a step above a 'Southern Negro'. He's protective of what he has.
- Crooks tries to uphold his pride and rights by asking Curley's wife to leave his room. However, she is quick to humiliate him and put him in his place. As she is a white woman, people will believe what she says over the words of a black man.

Quiz

1 Why does Curley's wife ask Lennie to feel her hair?   *2 pts*

    a She wants to make her husband jealous.

    b She wants to show Lennie how nice her hair is.

    c She wants Lennie to brush it for her.

2 How does Lennie kill Curley's wife?   *2 pts*

    a He throws her against a wall.

    b He stops her breathing with his hand.

    c He shakes her so hard her neck breaks.

3 Match the person to what they say about Curley's wife's death.   *4 pts*

Lennie **1**	**a** "You God damn tramp."
Candy **2**	**b** "George'll be mad."
George **3**	**c** "I'm gonna get 'im."
Curley **4**	**d** "I should of knew."

4 Carlson's gun is missing. What could have happened to it?   *2 pts*

    a Lennie has taken it.

    b George has taken it.

    c Carlson lost it somewhere.

1.b 2.c 3. 1=b, 2=a, 3=d, 4=c, 4. b

Your score
...../10 pts

Recap

When?	Sunday afternoon
Where?	A barn
Who?	• Lennie • Curley's wife • Candy • George • the other men of the ranch
What?	Lennie is in the barn, stroking his dead puppy, which he has accidentally killed. He is worried about telling George, as George might get angry and not let him keep rabbits in the future.
	Curley's wife appears. Lennie talks to her about why he likes stroking soft things like rabbits and she allows him to stroke her hair. She gets angry with him and he gets scared, holding her more tightly and then shaking her to silence her. However, this ends up killing her. Lennie remember George's instruction to meet at the river if he gets into trouble. He goes, leaving the body in the barn.
	Curley finds his wife's body. He tells George, who agrees they need to tell the other men. Curley, enraged and wanting Lennie dead, encourages the other men to go hunting for him. They agree and head out, leaving Candy alone with the body.

Key ideas

▷ **Regrets**
  • Curley's wife talks to Lennie about the opportunities she missed and the life she could have had as an actress. She compares this with her current unhappy marriage with Curley.
  • Lennie regrets killing the puppy and worries that he won't be allowed to have the rabbits he dreams of. He later regrets killing Curley's wife, again worried that he will get in trouble in the future. While he does not fully understand how difficult his situation is, he knows that he has done wrong.

▷ **Fatalism**
  • Candy's main reaction to the death of Curley's wife is anger and frustration that now he won't be able to join Lennie and George in setting up a farm. He knows that life hasn't changed, that he is still a cripple with no future.
  • George knows that he cannot travel with Lennie anymore and that their dream has gone. He now sees nothing in the future but working for a while, wasting the money, then travelling to find more work and starting again: a life with no hope.
  • Lennie is unable to look after himself and if he is caught, he might be hurt and would not survive prison. There seems to be no hope for the big man.

Quiz

1 Which of the following is *not* one of the visions that talks to Lennie? *2 pts*

ⓐ His mother

ⓑ His aunt Clara

ⓒ A rabbit

2 Lennie knows that George is going to shoot him. *2 pts*

☐ True ☐ False

3 Match the person to what they said. *4 pts*

Aunt Clara **①**   **ⓐ** "You remember ever' word I say."

George **②**   **ⓑ** "How'd you do it?"

Lennie **③**   **ⓒ** "I thought you was mad at me."

Carlson **④**   **ⓓ** "You never give a thought to George."

4 What did Slim mean by, "Never you mind. A guy got to sometimes."? *2 pts*

ⓐ George shouldn't have got involved in the situation.

ⓑ George should leave Lennie and go back to the ranch.

ⓒ George didn't have a choice. He had to do what he did.

1. a 2. false 3. 1=d, 2=a, 3=c, 4=b 4. c

Your score
...../10 pts

Recap

When?	Late Sunday afternoon
Where?	The bank of the river, as in Chapter 1
Who?	• Lennie • George • the other men of the ranch
What?	Lennie has gone back to the riverbank, as George had told him to. He is worried about what he has done and what George will say. Lennie sees two visions in his mind. First, his Aunt Clara appears, blaming him for what he has done. Then, a giant rabbit tells him that George will leave him alone. George arrives. He isn't angry with Lennie and they talk about their dream again. As they talk, George tells Lennie to look towards the distance and then he shoots Lennie in the back of the head. The other men arrive and George goes back to the ranch with Slim, who tells George he had no choice.

Key ideas

▶ **Loneliness**

- The rabbit tells Lennie that George will leave him all alone. This is clearly the greatest fear that Lennie has.
- George says that being alone would be much easier, because without Lennie he would have no trouble. However, it's clear he doesn't really mean this and would miss Lennie. Later, he also repeats the idea that if he were alone, he would waste his money and have no future.
- They talk about the importance of having someone else that cares about them: "we got each other, that's what". This makes George's decision and the ending of the novella all the more tragic.

▶ **Lies for a good purpose**

- George tells Lennie that their dream is still going to happen, so as to keep him calm and happy in his last few minutes.
- George lies to Carlson, saying that Lennie stole the gun.
- Slim understands what has happened and is prepared to back up George's actions. He will go along with the lie so that George does not get into trouble.

Boost your English

with Of Mice and Men

Language Games

1. **Guess which words are contracted in the words in bold in the table below.**

I **gotta** tell you again, do I?	
I **coulda** made something of myself.	
What **kinda** job?	
Leggo his hands, Lennie.	

2. **Rewrite the following sentences from *Of Mice and Men* in standard English, modifying the double negation (in bold).**

ⓐ He **ain't gonna** let me tend **no** rabbits.

....

ⓑ It **ain't nobody's** mouse.

....

ⓒ I **wasn't** doin' **nothing** bad with it, George.

....

ⓓ I wouldn't touch **none** of it.

....

3. **Below are some sentences that use idioms from *Of Mice and Men*. Fill in the blanks with the appropriate expression.**

| **look like hell** | **got in trouble** | **got the eye on [sth/so]** | **for God's sake** |

ⓐ He always .... in the mornings before he has a shower and drinks some coffee.

ⓑ I think I'm going to buy that book I've ....

ⓒ ...., don't do something as stupid as that!

ⓓ Both of them .... with their parents for it.

4 Pick the right meaning for each expression.

a If you blow your stake…

| A | you spend all your money. | B | you earn a lot of money. |

b If you roll up a stake…

| A | you spend a lot of money. | B | you save up some money. |

c If you bust a gut…

| A | you eat too much. | B | you engage in very difficult physical labour. |

d If you're in hot water…

| A | you are taking a hot bath. | B | you are in trouble. |

e If you're canned, this means…

| A | you are stuck at home and not able to go out. | B | you're fired. |

f If you have ants in your pants…

| A | you have a sexually transmitted infection. | B | you are nervous and restless. |

g If you shove off…

| A | you show that you are proud of what you've done. | B | you leave. |

h If you're flat bust…

| A | you're poor. | B | you're rich. |

Solutions:
4 a) A, b) B, c) B, d) B, e) B, f)
B, g) B, h) A

Language Games

⑤ Fit the following animals into the sentences from the book. Be careful with *singular* and *plural*.

rabbit bear pig louse salmon heron mule

ⓐ One of my lead .... got a bad hoof.

ⓑ An' when the .... run up river we could catch a hundred of 'em.

ⓒ It swam the length of the pool and came to the legs of a motionless .... that stood in the shallows.

ⓓ Says 'positively kills ...., roaches and other scourges.'

ⓔ He walked heavily, dragging his feet a little, the way a ...., drags his paws.

ⓕ We'll have a big vegetable patch and a .... hutch and chickens.

ⓖ When we kill a .... we can smoke the bacon and the hams.

⑥ Change the following sentences from the book into standard English.

Example: Any you boys seen Curley?   Have any of you boys seen Curley?

ⓐ I can't talk to nobody but Curley.   ....

ⓑ I ain't got nothing to do.   ....

ⓒ We gonna work on a ranch, George.   ....

ⓓ I seen him goin' in your house.   ....

ⓔ Le's get outa here.   ....

ⓕ I would of had to drowned most of 'em.   ....

7 Complete the following sentences using '*makes*', '*lets*', '*wants*', '*tells*' or '*asks*'.

ⓐ George .... to have his own farm.

ⓑ George .... Slim to give Lennie a puppy.

ⓒ George .... Lennie stop playing with the dead mouse.

ⓓ The boss .... George for his name.

ⓔ George .... Lennie to stop squeezing Curley's hand.

ⓕ George .... Lennie's name to the boss.

ⓖ Lennie often .... trouble.

ⓗ Curley's wife .... Lennie play with her hair.

8 Which of the following is not a possible meaning of 'ain't'.

ⓐ is not   **ⓑ** has not

ⓒ will not   **ⓓ** am not

9 Match the verbs to the appropriate nouns to make jobs on a farm.

to saddle ⓐ	❶ fences
to chop down ⓑ	❷ seeds
to repair ⓒ	❸ cattle
to pick ⓓ	❹ plants
to sow ⓔ	❺ a horse
to water ⓕ	❻ pesticides
to herd ⓖ	❼ trees
to spray ⓗ	❽ fruit

Solutions:
7 a) wants, b) asks, c) makes, d) asks, e) tells,
f) tells, g) makes, h) lets
8 c) will not
9 a) 5, b) 7, c) 1, d) 8, e) 2, f) 4, g) 3, h) 6

10 Lennie is described as a very big man, while George is a small man. Circle all the words similar to 'big' and underline all those similar to 'small'.

huge	medium	tiny	miniscule	average
	giant	massive	meager	runty
middling	hefty	bulky	pocket-sized	ordinary

11 Complete the following sentences, using an appropriate preposition.

after	down	forward/ahead	for	out	around

a Most men don't have anything to look .... to.

b George has looked .... Lennie for many years.

c I'm looking .... my wife. Have you seen her?

d Look .... or you'll mess up my hair!

e Carlson looked ...., trying to find his gun.

f As the boss's son, Curley looked .... on the farm workers.

12 Complete the following sentences with words related to the *hand*.

thumbs	knuckles	fingers	fist	wrist	fingernails

a George snapped his .... sharply to tell Lennie to give him the mouse.

b Curley's .... was lost in Lennie huge hand.

c Curley's wife had red ....

d Slim felt the dead woman's ...., looking for a pulse.

e The boss stood there, with his .... in his belt.

f Candy often rubs his beard with the .... of one hand.

⓭ Choose the correct meaning of these phrases:

ⓐ If you sock someone, you...

❶ fire them   ❷ hit them   ❸ insult them

ⓑ If you scram, you...

❶ run away   ❷ eat   ❸ make a mistake

ⓒ If you pitch a horseshoe, you...

❶ sell it   ❷ throw it   ❸ make it

⓮ Choose the correct word in the following sentences.

ⓐ You *might/must* as well come in and sit down.

ⓑ I don't have my work card! I *can't/must* have lost it.

ⓒ Crooks *might/can't* live with the other men because he's black.

ⓓ If you don't believe me, you *can/might* ask George.

ⓔ You *oughtn't/shouldn't* to be in here.

ⓕ If I'd gone, I *should/could* have been an actress.

My *Of Mice and Men*

My character map

My favorite character

....

....

....

The quotes I liked most

....
....
....
....
....
....
....
....

What I want to remember about this book

....
....
....
....
....
....
....
....
....

 Book**Advisor**

Plot
Did the story keep you hooked?

☆ ☆ ☆ ☆ ☆

Characters
Interesting profiles?

☆ ☆ ☆ ☆ ☆

Themes
Thought-provoking?

☆ ☆ ☆ ☆ ☆

Relevance
Does the story relate to anything going on today?

☆ ☆ ☆ ☆ ☆

Reading time
Did you race through the book?

☆ ☆ ☆ ☆ ☆

Language
Easy to read?

☆ ☆ ☆ ☆ ☆

Value
Is this book a good way to boost your English?

☆ ☆ ☆ ☆ ☆

Importance
Would you consider it a masterpiece?

☆ ☆ ☆ ☆ ☆

Your overall rating?
...../10 pts

Notes

 **Listen**

Maggie's Farm

Bob Dylan
1965

Rage Against the Machine (Cover)

2000

This is a song about the struggles of workers in America. In particular, it talks about low wages and poor treatment by bosses.

You're My Best Friend

Queen
1976

This song was written about the wife of one of the band members. However, the themes of needing and relying on another person mirror George and Lennie's relationship.

Somewhere Only We Know

Keane
2004

This English band sing about a dream, rather like Lennie's and George's. This, too, is a simple dream of a place only they know, a place they can rely on to give them hope.

 **Watch**

Of Mice and Men

Gary Sinise
1992

Sinise, who played George as well as directing the movie, was nominated for the Palme d'Or for his work on the film. It was widely praised by critics and sticks very closely to the novella's storyline.

The Shawshank Redemption

Franck Darabont
1994

A modern classic and one of the most beloved movies of the 1990s. It covers many of the same themes, including loneliness, powerlessness, race and what it means to have a dream.

Ironweed

Héctor Babenco
1988

Set in the 1930s Great Depression, this movie describes the lives of two homeless people. It stars the great actors Jack Nicholson and Meryl Streep.

 **Read**

The Grapes of Wrath

John Steinbeck
1939

This is Steinbeck's masterpiece and perhaps the main reason why he won the Nobel Prize. It is also set in California during the Great Depression, looking at the lives of traveling workers from Oklahoma. Beware! It's over 500 pages long!

To Kill a Mockingbird

Harper Lee
1962

Set in the Great Depression, this novel looks at race, class, injustice and the innocence of children. It is one of the most influential novels of all time.

Flowers for Algernon

Daniel Keyes
1966

A man with a low IQ, similar to Lennie, is given surgery to increase his intelligence. He sees the differences in his life and the ways people treat him, leading him to question if the surgery was an improvement or not.

Vous enseignez l'anglais ?

Un guide pédagogique est téléchargeable
gratuitement sur www.belin-education.com

Dans la même collection

The Importance of Being Earnest

Oscar Wilde

Creepy Stories

**The Tell-Tale Heart,
The Fall of the House of Usher
and other stories…**

Edgar Allan Poe

Animal Farm

George Orwell

7,90 €

**Envie de lire un autre classique
dans cette collection ?**

Envoyez-nous vos suggestions !

notsoclassic@humensis.com

Si votre proposition est retenue,
vous recevrez un exemplaire gratuit !